Chill Out & Stop Making This Weird:

A Girl's Survival Guide Extraordinaire

By Kelly Olson

Chill Out & Stop Making This Weird: A Girl's Survival Guide Extraordinaire

This is a work of fiction. Names, places, characters, and incidents are either used fictionally or are product of the author's imagination. Any resemblance to events, actual persons, living or dead, business establishments, or locales is entirely coincidental.

ISBN For this edition: 978-0-578-65513-0

All inquiries**: kellyolsonbooks@gmail.com**

Book formatting by: Last Mile Publishing

This book is dedicated
to the awkward kid
in all of us.

TABLE OF CONTENTS

CHAPTER ONE

Chickened Out

Let's be honest, we've all pulled the old run-the-thermometer-under-the-water trick to fake sick. Desperate times require desperate measures. It's not exactly a TikTok original, but at 6:02 AM my head is cemented to my pillow and my body refused to budge. Being coherent *and* original at 6:02 AM is technically impossible.

But today might be my lucky day. It is staff meeting Tuesday and mom tends to be a hot mess getting ready on Tuesdays. I don't get it, but she changes a hundred times in the mornings to find the *right* outfit for the staff meeting. Every week, she leaves a mountain of clothes and a buffet of shoes piled in front of her full-length bedroom mirror. She's a classic. It's like watching the same rerun every week. When it's down to the last second, she'll kick the clothes away from the mirror to make her final check while asking me what I think. No matter how retro she looks, I always confirm she's spot-on so we can finally get a move-on.

Today should play right into my master plan of staying home and Netflix binging while consuming Glamma's pink banana bread loaded with more sprinkles than the bread itself. Staff meeting Tuesdays might end up being my new favorite weekday.

This girl's staff meeting will consist of the Netflix remote, the couch, and a whole lot of pink banana bread. I deserve some Netflix therapy especially after this week's never-ending puberty unit at school. There has been a serious overdose of discussion about sanitary napkins, periods, tampons, breasts, virginia, hormones, peanuts, cramps, zits, and other nasty stuff.

I'll text my BFF, Shelby, and entice her to swing by after school for Glamma's famous pink banana bread and fill me in on what is on the test. Simple plan really. I'll take the test in peaceful solitude after school sometime later this week. Mom will never suspect anything because I am always the good kid that has never pulled *any* stunt.

I glanced at the time on my phone knowing Mom will summon me shortly to make Tuesday's outfit approval. I need to play it safe and at least make an appearance in order to keep her from getting suspicious.

I trudged into the bathroom, flipped on the light switch, and HOLY CYCLOPS! I grew a third eyeball overnight. I inched closer to the mirror for further inspection. Confirmed! A zit the size of Mount St. Helen dead center of my forehead. Nice.

It's official. I am absolutely *not* going to school today. A cyclops appearance would be a complete social disaster especially if Chet is in school today. Puberty review *and* Mount St. Helen is a solid no-show at school for this kid.

Exactly why didn't I pay attention when Mrs. Watson talked about acne care? Why couldn't I muster a glance at the slides? I have no problem watching Dr. Pimple Popper on TLC. I actually love that show, but I wasn't looking to make a special guest appearance.

OMGAWD! I need dramatic de-zit intervention help ASAP. What am I supposed to do with this massive red beast on my face? Why do I have such an aversion to understanding basic skin care? I confess, I have no zit care skill set whatsoever.

I quickly reached for my phone, opened my Pinterest app and typed *teen acne* into the search box. Several pictures of toothpaste showed up indicating application.

I quickly fumbled through my drawer in desperate search for the miracle mint paste and squeezed out a blob on my finger. I painted the sticky paste on the red swollen area. Nothing instantaneously happened other than the fresh minty scent now coming from my forehead.

Let's be honest, this whole turning twelve thing is not for me. Growing a third eyeball overnight and people expecting me to act more maturely is grossly overrated.

Last night at dinner, mom and I were talking about what I wanted to do for my upcoming birthday and about me turning another year older. I thought it was as good a time as any to tell her how I feel totally young on thc insidc.

Mom said that everyone does. She is in her late thirties and mom said she feels like she's in her early twenties on the inside, but not on the outside. She rambled on about her crow's feet, saggy knee skin, that her upper lip disappeared somewhere, and other weird stuff that shows her *real* age.

Who even knew that knees sagged, or crows landed by your eyes? I've never witnessed any birds landing on her face or even swarm her for that matter. Sounds a little drama mama-ish.

Maybe everyone actually feels younger on the inside. Is there actually a day when your inside age matches your outside age?

I can't imagine my Glamma, who refuses to be called grandma, feeling like she's younger on the inside. Who knows? *She* probably does. After all, she does have a sincere obsession with bedazzling EVERYTHING SHE OWNS with plastic rhinestone jewels using the Bedazzle gun that she bought on TV. She claims it is the best invention of all time.

Glamma has bedazzled her jean jackets, glasses, flip-flops, hats, jeans, purses, you name it. I always thought she was *original.* I should ask her what her inner age is. I'm guessing somewhere between seven and eight, based on her never-ending, blinged out attire and endless excitable energy.

Facts are facts and my very mature eleven-year-old self knows for certain that Netflix and keeping Mount St. Helen from erupting trumps Mrs. Watson's tampon review talk *any* day.

Mom yelled upstairs, "Maddie, you need to hustle, honey. I have a staff meeting at school today. Remember? We need to leave earlier than usual, and I wanted your thoughts on this outfit."

I replied, "I'm coming, Mom." I threw on some random clothes from my floor and dashed downstairs to mom's bathroom.

I ravaged through mom's makeup drawer until I found her concealer stick. I popped the cap and carefully dabbed over the toothpaste concealing everything with an even coat of skin colored liquid. I threw the stick back in her drawer, approved her outfit, grabbed my backpack and slid in the backseat of the car.

Yup, I succumbed to yet another hurry up, get in the car, rat race before I even realized it. Locked in the car, jammed next to Pesty Peyton in the backseat, and soon to be locked into the puberty review.

It figures, I chickened out of the whole fake thermometer thing. As usual. All talk, no action.

CHAPTER TWO

The Anonymous Puberty Question Box

Mrs. Watson, our cool fashion blogger teacher, greeted each one of us at the door as we entered the classroom.

"Good morning! I am so glad that you are here Maddie." Mrs. Watson said invitingly. I know the drill. I have two options both coming into the classroom in the morning and exiting in the afternoon; throw up a high five or get a hug to get through the door. Ninety nine percent of the time, I go for the hug.

Wayne, who fondly calls himself Wayniac, a name combo of Wayne + maniac, rammed into my back as he tried to slide through the door behind me to avoid contact with Mrs. Watson. She put down her arm like the crossing arm on a school bus.

She flashed Wayne a smile and said, "Wayne, my day wouldn't be the same without seeing your big smile." Wayniac beamed from ear to ear threw her a high five and darted into the classroom searching for Titan, his partner in crime.

Today, I was in the one percent club for fear of getting concealer on Mrs. Watson's beautiful coral suit jacket. I high fived her and made my way to my assigned seat and dropped a pile of homework and a smashed Twinkie on my desk. Sarah looked at me an abnormally long time and finally said, "Maddie, I think you accidently got some toothpaste or food or something on your forehead. You might want to wipe it off."

I coolly replied, "Oh, geez, my bad." I wiped it off on my forearm. Great, now my head is red and my arm is brownish green and minty fresh. Good start.

Sarah gave me an oddly approving look and then asked, "Did you study for the puberty test?"

"Not at all." I replied, "Did you?"

Sarah continued, "No, I was planning on getting up early to study, but my alarm never went off."

"We are in the same boat then. I'm just glad this is the last day of it."

"I know, right?" Sarah replied.

Mrs. Watson closed the door and instructed, "Will everyone please take your seat? We are taking a break from our morning journal because we have so much to cover with trying to wrap up our Puberty Unit today." Low sighs filled the room.

She quickly sat down at her computer and proceeded with daily roll call. The only names that I seem to hear every day are Chet's and mine. I verbally respond to mine and I find myself writing *Mrs. Chet Johnson* on the inside cover of my notebook over and over after I hear his name being called out. I have written it in every colored pen, in cursive, in squiggly letters, block letters, you name it, I have created it. Today, I decided to start in the back of my notebook cover and change it up a bit; *Chet & Maddie Johnson.* It has a nice ring to it.

"For a quick review, can someone tell me what this is called and how it aids in menstruation?" Mrs. Watson asked from her podium as she held up a pink plastic tubular thing in one hand and a cotton wad looking thing with a string hanging down from it in the other. I quickly threw my notebook in my desk and sat studiously quiet.

Silence. Dead Silence.

"Well, these are a few of the feminine hygiene products called tampons. They are used to absorb the menstrual flow by insertion into the vagina during menstruation. Some come with various colored plastic applicators such as this," she paused and held up the pink plastic thing and continued, "which gets discarded upon insertion and others do not come with applicators," and she held up the other hand.

Mrs. Watson proceeded to demonstrate and pushed the skinnier end of the plastic applicator into the bigger end of the pink applicator. Clearly, she applied too much force because the cotton section with the string dangling from it shot out of the end of the plastic applicator through the air like a party popper shooting out confetti. The tampon landed on Garrett's desk and bounced off toward his tennis shoe.

Garrett ejected out of his chair and yelled in his high-pitched cracking voice, "WATSON! What the heck are you doing? Are you trying to kill me?"

"Oh, Garrett, I am sooo sorry. I didn't mean to push it all the way, but it must have stuck. I am so sorry." Mrs. Watson replied as she bent over to pick up the evidence.

Sarah leaned in, "LOL, flying tampons? Pretty sure Garrett has PTSD now."

We started to giggle which became infectious. Except for pale faced Garrett, of course. Definitely, a not-funny-*now* moment for him. Epic, but def not funny to him.

After the rumble settled, all eyes were highly vigilant on Watson's demonstrations for flying objects with solid goals to stay off the puberty radar at all costs.

Mrs. Watson pulled more tricks out from behind the podium. "Okay, no shooting parts with these, I promise."

She lined various pads on her wooden podium. "These are four kinds of sanitary napkins. Also known as pads. They have one sticky side that is affixed to a female's panties and the other side is used as an absorbent during menstruation. Sanitary pads are also used after giving birth and for various surgeries."

Mrs. Watson removed a paper-like strip and stuck one to her podium demonstrating the sticky side. OMG.

"Both pads and tampons need to be changed based on the intensity of the menstrual flow. Nonetheless, they should be changed at least every three to four hours and discarded properly as we discussed last week."

Full disclosure, I would *never* openly admit that I generally enjoy school. Watson usually keeps it pretty lighthearted and fun. I'm not only referring to when she fuels us with candy. Don't get me wrong, candy is a definite plus, but it's more than that.

However, today is an entirely different story because this isn't anything close to *fun.* There is a major disconnect between how Mrs. Watson is standing in front of the class talking about tampons and pads like she's talking about improper fractions or something. The only thing improper here is talking about tampons and sticky pads. I don't get it *at all.* That is not a 'thing.' You can't roll that kind of info out the same way you would teach math without any influx in voice, awkward nonverbal twitches, or avoiding eye contact with the people standing right in front of you.

I'm pretty sure that Mrs. Watson didn't leave *anything* out. She went from one landmine to the next. She discussed tampons, pads, public hair, reproduction, armpit hair, shaving, changing voices, facial hair, breasts, and then *bras*...

Did she just say, "bras?" Call 911 right now! I'm definitely going into cardiac arrest. This has gone too far. Bras? It has never even once crossed my mind that I would *wear* a bra. If I *ever* had to put a bra on, it would roll right up to my chin at roller coaster speed like a pull-down window shade springing up and whipping around the top rod. Why? Because there isn't anything to hold down the cuppy mini hammock looking thingys that get strapped on to the front of our body that they call a bra. There is no overhang happening on my chest whatsoever to anchor *anything* down.

Realizing that no one rushed into the classroom with white jackets, a first-aid emergency responder kit, or a stretcher, I resorted to the only survival technique left. I folded my hands nicely on my desk and did the stone face stare straight ahead and watched the secondhand tick on the front wall clock. No one has ever claimed survival to be entertaining.

This is the only sure way to avoid *all* eye contact. I don't want Mrs. Watson to catch my eye and think that she can engage me with a question and I certainly can't possibly have eye contact with a boy.

I'd love to pull out a magic remote and push the fast forward button on Mrs. Watson's mouth. If I could only hyper speed the process and see her lips move frantically and then hear her say the most pleasing words on the face of the earth, "Now that concludes our Puberty Unit." If only.

But noooooo, I slowly suffered through it constantly asking myself why I am such a rule follower. I envisioned myself horizontal on the couch with a real remote in my hand eating superman ice cream straight out of the carton and stuffing myself with Glamma bread. Such a rebel… in my daydreams. Ugh.

Suddenly, there was a shift in Mrs. Watson's disposition. She went over to the obnoxious neon yellow Puberty Question Box sitting on her desk as if she was going to announce the winner of the Grammy's or something. She cleared her throat and shot us a half grin kind of look, like the Grinch when he's going to do something suspicious.

Well, hopefully this is over. I tune in intently.

Finally, Mrs. Watson said, "Now, I will look in the Puberty Question Box to see if there are any more anonymous questions that any of you put in there before I hand out the test after lunch today."

She pulled out a piece of crumpled up paper with a question scribbled on it and after a long pause, read it aloud: "Can girls have wet dreams like boys do?"

WHAAAAATTTT?!

Who put *that* question in the box? Wet dreams? Did I miss something along the way? What the heck is a wet dream? Was that thrown in somewhere when we were talking about the differences between tampons and pads when I was having a stare down with the wall clock? How can she even answer this question and still have a job tomorrow? What is happening? Have we all lost our minds during this Puberty Unit? Come on, people. Let's keep it together. We are almost through this. Hasn't anyone ever heard of Google before? Why would someone put this question in The Box? Just Google it!

Mrs. Watson's eyes scanned the classroom as if she was going to call on someone to answer the question. My body flushed with intense heat and my breathing resembled a dog pant. My mind kept flashing RUN! RUN! The only way out of this is to make a fast break for the bathroom.

Then there was a sound coming from Mrs. Watson's mouth. She coolly rolled out, "This is a very good question, and it's part of the curriculum to teach about nocturnal emissions, or in other words, wet dreams. Girls don't ejaculate so they don't have wet dreams in the same way that boys do."

Now, that's some serious relief.

Finally, *one* thing that I don't have to worry about. I'm so freaked out already about

#1. WHEN is my period coming?

#2. WHY all the mystery with the start date? Why can't I know and put it on my Google calendar?

My anxiety has peaked. It is at an all-time high. And to add to all of this, I sit next to the HOTTIE OF HOTS, Chet Johnson. He makes me melt just by looking at him. Not to mention the times when his hand brushes mine when he passes out papers or hands me something and our eyes lock. I nearly pass out every time.

I feel really bad that Chet has to sit here and suffer through understanding a pad, tampon, and length of a period.

I admit it is annoying that boys never have to go through any of that stuff, but it's wrong that they are sitting in here with us.

They don't need to understand that a pad has one sticky side to adhere to your underwear and how to properly dispose of one of the ten million varieties of pads nor do they need to understand the difference between a built-in applicator and a non-applicator tampon. It's useless information for them and this needs serious reform.

I'm barely making it. Imagine the boys? They have to be somewhat relieved that they don't *have* to deal with a period one week every month for forty-plus years until some unknown *magical* day when you are old, and it stops for good. I guess they call it *menopause* when it stops forever. I sure hope it doesn't actually *pause*, but it actually stops. It should be called *menostop*, not menopause. Dah.

I'm boycotting this whole menstruation/period thing. I'm just not doing it.

I don't see any upside. Not doing it. Plain and simple.

I'm going with mind over matter on this particular life event. My mind decided to veto this matter in my life. Just like that. I'm skipping it. I'm doing one huge leapfrog over it.

Why deal with cramps and hauling around the small, cutesy bag of pads and/or tampons like nobody knows what's in there? Carrying around the cutesy bag is like carrying around a flashing neon sign that says, "Hey, look! I'm having my period!"

Not doing it.

I mean, I *am* mature already. I don't need a messy process to prove it. Period.

A soft knock at the classroom door snapped me back to Room 106. Mrs. Watson opened the door and found Mrs. Zooba, the school nurse, standing in the doorway with her hair loosely piled on top of her head, smacking her gum, while balancing two large boxes on her knee. Mrs. Watson quickly rescued the potential landslide by grabbing the top box.

"Good morning, Mrs. Zooba, what a nice surprise. Please come in." Mrs. Watson welcomed her.

"What did you bring us today?" Mrs. Watson asked.

Mrs. Zooba set the other box down while attempting to fix the mess on top of her head. She replied, "I have some parting bags for your students for the completion of your Puberty Unit. The blue bags are for the boys and the pink bags are for the girls. Each of them contains products and coupons for things that they will need during their pubescent years."

Pubescent? Really.

Mrs. Zooba continued, "You can take your bags and open them later if you'd like because they are all the same. Boys will receive deodorant, nail kits, shaving cream, and some coupons for shavers. Girls, you will receive deodorant, shaving cream, nail kits, pads, tampons, and coupons for other feminine products."

Oh, my gawd! This bag is hitting the trashcan ASAP. I would not be caught dead with this. Well maybe I'll grab the mini deodorant out of the gift bag first.

A *gift bag*? Did she say gift bag? It's not exactly the party-favor *gift* bag I am accustomed to, but nevertheless, I'll salvage the mini deodorant and maybe the nail kit, but that's it. I'll dispose of all traces of pad and tampon evidence immediately. Wait, did she say parting bag? Who knows, it's all weird no matter how she said it.

The lunch bell rang, and we all got up and walked to the lunchroom like muted zombies. I can't remember a day when we didn't get in trouble for being too loud in the hallway from Marge-the-Sarge, short for sergeant, hall monitor. I guess the grand finale wet dream question along with the party favors left us utterly speechless. It's just too much.

CHAPTER THREE

Lying Non-Perioder

We robotically went through the lunch line. It never matters what you throw on your beige plastic lunch tray because all prison food tastes like the same cardboard.

The awkward, subdued nature of all of us carried over to the lunch table.

It was as if some puberty rain cloud followed us out of our classroom, down the hall, and into the lunchroom. I caught myself looking down the lunch table bench, wondering if any of the girls already had their period. Panic struck my non-budding chest like a lightning bolt. What if…what if all the girls were already having their periods and I was the *only* one who hasn't?

Instantly, I felt like I was sucker punched right in the gut as I was gnawing on my cheese melted over cardboard pizza. Do you know what a sucker punch is? It's when someone hits you and you don't see it coming. It's like a cheap shot. Not that I've actually ever had one, but I imagine it to feel like I do right now. I took note of the bra strap cinching down on Brianna, Mia, and Brooke's shoulders. I saw Haley had a hot pink bra strap peeking out of her shirt collar. I also noted that Mia went to the girl's bathroom today with a little cosmetic bag. Could that be her *bag* of period stuff?

I remembered Mrs. Watson said that it wasn't scientifically proven, but girls tend to start their periods around the same time that their biological mothers did.

Now, this wasn't exactly a topic of conversation that my mom and I have ever casually chatted about, but I need to know the answer to this question--just in case vetoing going through puberty is a hard fail. I can hardly wait to ask her this question. Not.

How do I even start that conversation? *So, Mom, I was just wondering… when did you get your period? Ugh.*

Then there it was. Dropped from the sky like an atomic bomb hit the lunch table.

"Maddie, have you had your period yet?" someone asked from the *other* end of the mile-long lunch table.

"Um, me?" I responded, like a dork.

Everyone at the table had laser vision on my face as they waited for an answer and a reaction.

I hesitated.

I hunched my shoulders forward, creating a tent-like effect over my chest so no one could see if I had a bra on or even a chest, for that matter.

Of course, I didn't have a bra on. I didn't even own one. What would be the purpose?

I don't need one *or do I?* Complete nausea set in. I started sweating profusely, my eyebrows shot up suddenly feeling like I was five years old compared to some of the girls at the table. Instantly, I realized that some of my friends looked like they could be sixteen.

"Yaaaa," I blurted out.

Okay, that was too long of a hold on the *a* to seem believable.

Why did I say yes? Total choking guilt.

Oh, for the curse of puberty!

How am I going to get out of this totally stupid, no-upside lie?!

Not only have I not experienced a period, now I'm a *lying Non-Perioder!*

I don't even have a *bag* to fake it.

Hurry!

Think fast, Maddie.

Provide full disclosure.

Now.

Stop this insanity before it goes any further.

I felt like I was going to puke up this mystery-meat pizza.

Mia looked at me and said, "Don't you just hate having your period?"

I forced back regurgitating the cardboard with all my might.

Okay, well based on the fact that I have NEVER experienced it, I was clueless as to what to say.

Do I just keep this lie going and say, "Yes" with an Elvis lip and a flip of my hair over my shoulder, or do I tell the entire lunch table that I've never actually had it?

I, being the lamest, immature almost twelve-year-old, did neither.

I looked blankly down the table in her direction.

I was so conflicted. I desperately want to be a member of The Period Club, which I didn't even know existed until now.

This exact statement is what my dad has pounded in my head my whole life:

Integrity=doing what is right, even when it's hard.

This definitely fits in the hard category.

Why does the doing what is right part have to be SO stinking difficult?

Why can't I just be cool, for once?

"Actually, I haven't had mine yet" I said softly, letting the words roll off my tongue.

"Really? I thought you said that you did?" Mia said persistently.

"Welcome to my club, Maddie. I haven't had mine either," Sarah interjected.

"Well, I'd rather be a part of that club any day than The Period Club we're in, right Mia?" Haley piped in.

Just then, Zach and Chet squeezed in between Haley and I on the bench. They picked the pepperonis off our pizza and popped them in their mouths like popcorn.

"Get out of here, you're annoying." Haley pushed on Zach's shoulder.

"No, seriously girls, I was wondering if I could cheat off your puberty test when we get back to the room. My mom threatened to enroll me in some weird Family-Life class this summer if I bomb this unit. It's literally game over for me if you guys don't help me." Zach begged.

"The last thing I'm going to do is get caught cheating on the puberty test. Can you imagine that phone call home or the consequences associated with that crime?" Haley replied wide-eyed.

I sat there speechless because my hip was touching Chet's hip and my mind just went mush. This has never happened to me. I *always* have something to say, especially to annoying boys picking at my food.

The lunch bell rang and summoned us back to the classroom. Everyone moaned as they slowly drug themselves out of their seat, emptied their lunch tray, and meandered down the hall.

As we entered the room, Mrs. Watson was placing the puberty test on our desks.

"Welcome back. When you are finished with the test, please put it in the top tray on my desk, take a piece of candy from the jar, and use the rest of the time until everyone is finished for homework."

I sat down and got right to work. I'll be the first to admit, some of the questions on the test were completely foreign to me. Did Mrs. Watson give us the right test? I looked around to see if this was a universal thought. The only other person looking up was an unusually pale Zach who kept rolling his pencil back and forth over his test.

What is an STD and how do you get one? What is the only 100% way not to become pregnant and not get an STD? Um, are those trick questions? Did we go over these topics?

Oh no, what if *I* don't pass this unit? Would mom make *me* retake it with Zach this summer? Living through it once was awful. Twice would tip me over.

At this point, I do my best and hope that the odds of getting the correct answer on some of the multiple-choice questions are in my favor. I hand the test in.

The results will be available tomorrow. I'm just glad that it's *over,* for now anyway.

CHAPTER FOUR

Project Schmodject

When Zach waved the white flag and finally handed in his test, we knew work time was over. Mrs. Watson went to the front of the room and moved her podium to the corner. Then she pushed a long table in the front center of the room.

She cleared her throat and stated, "I know all of you have been looking forward to presenting your Personal Care Projects. As a reminder, it is twenty percent of your grade for this unit. Is there a group that would like to kick it off?"

Hardly. I guarantee there was not one kid in the entire room that was *looking forward to presenting* their Personal Care Project. Not one.

"Okay, why don't we start with your group, Emma?" Mrs. Watson suggested with a smile.

Emma waved to her group as to signal that they had no *real* choice and let's-just-get-this-done kinda wave.

Emma wrote NUTRITION on the whiteboard. Her group clumsily lined up clear glass jars filled and individually labeled Captain Crunch, Fruity Pebbles, Dunkin glazed doughnut, Pop Tart, and four more jars each labeled sugar.

Liam assembled a sugar jar next to each of the other labeled jars and asked, "Who eats sugar for breakfast?"

About half of the students proudly raised their hands. Emma walked around with snack baggies of sugar cubes and placed them on each person's desk.

"Each jar of sugar represents the amount of sugar in one serving of Captain Crunch, Fruity Pebbles, a Pop Tart, or a glazed Dunkin doughnut. Who would have guessed that there is more sugar in cereal than in a doughnut? There is over an eighth cup of sugar in one serving of Captain Crunch. That's insane!" exclaimed Garrett.

Liam flashed various sugar charts on the whiteboard and explained, "A lot of cereals contain as much or sometimes more than fifty percent sugar. There are far better options with less sugar that are full of protein and vitamins like eggs, fruit, and peanut butter toast for breakfast. My hockey coach always stressed input equals output for our body. So, tomorrow when you get up ask yourself if you want to *input* that bag of sugar cubes or fuel your body with healthy stuff and have the *output* be feeling great with energy that lasts all day."

"Well, done Nutrition group! Next week we will be talking about heart disease and diabetes and I will refer back to your awesome visuals to connect these two topics. Thank you so much team Nutrition. Everyone, give them a hand," encouraged Mrs. Watson.

Everyone systematically applauded as Wayniac reached over and grabbed my bag of sugar cubes and started throwing them in the air and catching them in his extra wide mouth. I was going to ask Chet if he wanted mine, but I guess he's sweet enough already and it doesn't really matter now because Wayniac had thrown them all down anyway.

"Next, will be the Grooming group." Mrs. Watson announced.

The Grooming group meandered to the front of the room. A few of them haphazardly organized what appeared to be a toiletry bag, a fingernail clipper, and a pen-like object with a long cap on the front table.

Noah fidgeted with something else with his back to the class while John wrote *NOSE HAIR, UNIBROW, and GNARLY NAILS* in large letters across the board.

When John finished writing, Noah whirled around sporting long black hair taped under his nose and a few straggler hairs taped to his ears. Everyone nervously laughed as a room of elbows slowly lifted to desktops and hands strategically rested under their noses concealing any potential unknown hairy nostrils.

"Have you ever noticed when someone has serious hair growing out of their nose or maybe even on their ear lobes? You may have noticed your grandpa with especially long nose hair, bushy eyebrows, or ear hair. Well guys, I am here to tell you that nose hair does not discriminate nor does the stuff that gets hung up in it. The good news is that all of this is easily manageable."

"Ewwww," echoed throughout the room.

Zach pulled a short curved scissors out of a toiletry bag and said, "Never pluck your nose hair because that can lead to an infection, not to mention it would hurt like crazy and would make any grown man's eyes water. All you need to do is trim your nose hair with a curved scissors that doesn't have a sharp end like this one. Another option is you could purchase a small pen-like shaver that runs on two AA batteries like this Wahl brand shaver. It makes the job super easy and it works well for trimming up your nose and around your ear lobes if you need it." Zach showed an image of the pen-like shaver on the white board. "Target sells these for less than ten dollars. Trust me, it's the way to go. Invest. You can all thank me later."

Steve switched to an image of a giant black unibrow on the screen. Kids slowly transitioned their hands to rest on their forehead as they gave a courtesy chuckle.

Steve said, "You could use a Wahl pen-like shaver to trim your unibrow or you can do it the old fashion way and use a tweezers and pluck the hair between your brows. Don't go crazy people, because that would look weird too." He flashed another image of someone who went a little too wild and plucked their eyebrows about two miles apart on their forehead.

"Maybe, some of us don't want to shave or pluck any body hair." Matt's voice half-jokingly shot out from the back of the room.

"No worries, because it's a personal choice and you do you. At the end of the day, no one really cares, but you. However, if you happen to be someone who would like to know a safe and correct procedure for eyebrow plucking, we provided a YouTube link for Mrs. Watson to send out once she approves it. Keep a look-out for it all you unibrowers that need some guidance," said Noah. Almost everyone reached for their forehead to feel if they had one or two brows. Of course, all I could feel was zit mountain. Well, at least it didn't feel like a furry mountain. I have that going for me.

Mia immediately stepped up to the whiteboard and wrote NAIL CARE. Simultaneously elf-like assistants passed around small Styrofoam bowls filled with warm sudsy water. Mia kinda looks like Ellen DeGeneres with her short blonde hair, striking blue eyes, and original style. I was waiting for her to say, "Now all of you feel under your seat. One of you will have an all-expense paid trip to a spa in Bora Bora. The rest of you will receive a new car to drive to your local spa for special treatment." But no, she actually isn't Ellen. She's Mia in Room 106 trying to survive this unit just like the rest of us.

Mia instructed, "Please grab the nail kit out of the bag that Mrs. Zooba provided us earlier today, set it on your desk, and then rest your fingernails in the soapy warm water for five minutes."

As I soaked my hands, I had a strong urge to grab my phone and flip the camera around to scope out if I had any stray nose hairs hanging out. I have never, not even one time in my ENTIRE life checked out my nose hair. OMG, why hasn't anyone ever mentioned this to me? Mom? Glamma? Watson? Total fail.

The group rambled on about only cutting nails straight across or something and they said something else about trimming hangnails. I couldn't really concentrate because I was too occupied trying to find something reflective in my desk to do a nose hair spot check.

The next group called to the front all sported hunter orange bandanas on their heads and they all had tennis shoes on. Parker chicken scratched the words BORED, LOW ENERGY, STRESSED, FEELING SAD, AND THROWING DOWN TOO MANY FLAMING DORITOS. Parker spun around like he was trying out for an infomercial. He threw his two pointer fingers at us like some used car salesman and said, "Well, I have a fun solution for you!" He spun back around and scribbled, *60 MINUTES/DAY* on the whiteboard.

"Every teen should exercise at least sixty minutes per day." Parker stated. With that that Brooke loudly blew the whistle that was hanging around her neck.

She commanded, "Everyone get up and follow me in a single line, keep up, no lolly-gaggers, no talking, no Snap Chatting, keep your hands to yourself, or we will turn this squad right around. We are going for a *PUMP-YOU-UP* power walk. We were given strict requirements for being allowed access to highly protected areas. Don't mess it up."

The drill sergeant swung open the door and we obediently marched out of the classroom in single file line at top speed. My calculated shuffle landed me a spot directly behind Chet. Full attention ahead.

I have no idea how Brooke got all this clearance, but we sped walked through the school kitchen as the hairnet adorned lunch ladies prepared our mush and chatted about their latest Pinterest craft and joyfully bragged about their grandkids. I'm always amazed how they can crank out over four hundred meals in less than ninety minutes five days a week so casually. I'm totally challenged making instant ramen noodles in the microwave. I must admit though, I have perfected making a mean vanilla wafer frosting sandwich.

From there we were whisked off to the principal's office. As far as I know, everything seemed par for a principal's office. It's not that I frequent the place or anything, but for the most part, it seemed basic. There was your standard desk lamp, two stiff beige chairs facing the desk, yellowed motivational signs covered the walls, and dusty dried flowers in a purple vase next to a framed picture of Wayniac on the credenza.

Wait. Wayniac? How did he make the credenza and no one else did? Strange. I'm not sure if it should be a goal to make the credenza or not to make the credenza. I'm going to stick with the latter, seems best to keep a low profile around here.

Brooke shot us out of the principal's office and passed secretary Ratburn's desk on the way out of the front office. We all generously helped ourselves to Mrs. Ratburn's complimentary bowl of leftover Halloween candy. Don't let the name scare you. She is as sweet as apple pie. All the kids love her. She's the heart of our school. Mom said that the most important people in the school besides all the cool kids are the secretaries and the maintenance staff. So, I am always extra nice to them.

Brooke whipped into the phy-ed teacher's office and skidded halfway across the floor. She nearly made a full-face plant onto the remains of an old McDonald's fries box lying next to a trash can. She immediately stopped the class train throwing her palm up. She rearranged her ponytail, picked up the smashed fry mess along with a half-eaten, giant size Snicker bar, launched them into the trash can, and sternly rerouted us to the maintenance room.

Dan-the-maintenance-man is the coolest guy. He had Christmas lights strung back and forth over his workshop illuminating his meticulously organized tools, labeled drawers, and his hundred rolls of duct tape lined up perfectly according to size and color. Dan-the-maintenance-man sat on his swivel workbench stool whistling to country music while happily repairing a student desk. Pictures of his family filled every open spot in his small work area. He shot us a gentle smile as we silently marched through.

Past Dan's cheerful work zone was the school stage and beyond that was a heavy black door that led into the dressing room. My entire life I have always wanted to sit at a Hollywood style makeup mirror and there were four of them right in front of my very eyes. Each of them had big, bright, round bulbs framing the mirrors and stacks of small makeup suitcases piled next to them. Isabelle nudged me in the back to keep moving. I looked ahead to see if Chet was still in front of me, but I must have gotten passed up when I geeked out over the full-on Hollywood set right there in WK Middle School. Who knew?

Not wanting to fall into last place, I sprinted past the racks of costumes that lined the walls which eventually led down to a dark metal stairwell. I grabbed the cold handrail snugly while trying to exhale the mustiness out of my nostrils and the thought of centipedes scurrying all over my body out of my head. I didn't want to show my intense fear of bugs and darkness, so I kept an unusually fast pace as we descended deeper into a dimly lit school dungeon space. The pathway slowly twisted until we came to a dead end where each person systematically took turns climbing rungs of a ladder and then *Presto*! Each of us popped out of a hidden trap door. We were on center stage with the lights shining down on us like rock stars.

So cool, but not something I would like to repeat any time soon.

Wayniac started having a slight melt down about how Brooke revealed his best hiding spot in school to e.v.e.r.y.o.n.e. Wasting no time addressing Wayniac's hissy fit, Brooke charged on to the art supply room that dripped with all sorts of glitter containers, blank canvases, tubs of clay and slime.

Brooke's nose twitched and suddenly she was off like a bloodhound trailing a severely burned popcorn waif. Her expert sniffer led us directly to Mr. Noll, a fourth-grade teacher. He was standing in front of the microwave in the teacher's lounge like a failed chef holding a smoldering bag of popcorn. He tore open the crispy charred bag and sheepishly offered us his overcooked kernels.

Brooke immediately responded for all of us, "Thank you Mr. Noll, but we are close to mission completion and we can't stop for snacks, maybe another time. Enjoy your lunch."

She marched straight across the hall into nurse Zooba's army barracks. Military style cots lined thc room with itchy wool blankets neatly folded on the end of each cot. The stiff cots were separated by peach colored curtains whose sole job was to keep the permanent vomit scent in and kids out.

Finally, Brooke kicked up the speed and we whisked down the hall, back into our room, and we collapsed in our chairs.

Looking at her watch, Brooke, heavily breathing, stated, "Now, you only have a minimum of forty-two minutes left to exercise today."

"If you shake up your exercise routine and try new activities or relocate your old activities like we just did, time flies and it's way more fun. Grab a friend and exercise with someone. Two is better than one." Brooke hit a button on the screen and flashed a list of ideas to change up our exercise. FOOT GOLF, HIKING, PICKLEBALL, BIKING, GOAT YOGA, HOME VIDEO EXERCISE, TENNIS, WALKING, FOOTBALL, BASKETBALL, BASEBALL, HOCKEY, SOCCER, VOLLEYBALL, DISC GOLF, DANCE, SWIMMING, PADDLEBOARDING, KAYAKING, SNOWSHOEING, CROSS COUNTRY SKIING, DOWNHILL SKIING, and more. She blew her whistle and sat down.

"Wow, that is what we need every day around here." Mrs. Watson expressed. "I will try to break up our day and do some Pump-You-Up power walks in and around our building. Thank you so much Exercise group. I loved it!"

"Now that we are recharged, how about we have our Skin Care group present?"

Wayniac walked directly to the front of the room and wrote ZIT in huge red letters across the entire board. IF my face and cyclops appears on the screen, I will erupt. I decided to slide out to the restroom as CJ and Skylar pulled out a washcloth, a bottle, and a small pouch like thing and set them on the table.

Upon my delayed return, my group was gathering at the front of the room with an extra-large bag of cotton balls and a few rubbery prickly balls. I scurried to the front and took my position.

I wrote FRIENDSHIP on the board in big pink letters. Under it I wrote SCREEN TIME, ACTIVITIES TO DO TOGETHER, SUMMER BUCKET LIST, GROUP TEXT, EXERCISE.

Conveniently, Chet McDreamy was in my group. He took over and explained, "Okay, each student will start with ten cotton balls. When you do or say something nice to someone, you spread warm fuzzies. When you do that, you hand them one cotton ball and the exchange continues throughout the day. The goal is to try to hand out all of your cotton balls even the ones that you receive throughout the day."

Shelby walked around and handed out the cotton balls. Chet said to Shelby, "Shelby, why are you so slow at handing those out?"

I threw Chet one of the purple rubber prickly balls and he caught it. I explained to the class, "You will get tossed the *cold* prickly ball if you say or do something negative. Just set it on your desk after you catch it. Hopefully, the cold prickly balls won't move off of the podium today. That should be our goal every day."

Shelby pointed to the list on the board and said, "Kids between the ages of eight to eighteen have an average screen time of seven hours a day. It is recommended that kids this age have a two-hour maximum daily screen time. Increased screen time has been linked to increased anxiety and depression."

Major eye rolls.

"I know I sound like some SiriusXM parental radio commercial or something, but I do know that personally, I feel a lot happier on days when I have some friend time. I think the key is to figure out how to make it less work and more fun to get together."

Logan stepped forward and stated, "The hardest part for most of us is the asking part. Sometimes you don't have the energy to put into organizing a get together and other times you fear rejection if someone thinks your idea is lame."

"That's true Logan, and that is why the exercise group gave us some fun healthy options to do together. Our group expanded on that and made another list of ideas. Don't let either of these lists hinder your own creativity. We suggest you devise your own fun bucket lists together. Utilize group texts for easy communication and be open to trying new things. Just be kind to each other, spread warm fuzzies, and make fun stuff happen." I explained as I flashed a list of ideas on the whiteboard.

START A FANTASY FOOTBALL LEAGUE, MAKE A MUSIC VIDEO, HOST A BEAN BAG TOURNAMENT, PLAY BOOT HOCKEY, VOLUNTEER, GO GEOCACHING, MAKE SLIME, HAVE A FONDUE PARTY, BUILD A SNOW FORT AND HAVE A SNOWBALL FIGHT, SET UP AN OUTDOOR MOVIE, MAKE HOMEMADE DOUGHNUTS, START A WATER GUN OR WATER BALLOON FIGHT, PLAY MINI GOLF, HAVE A HULA HOOP COMPETITION, MAKE A NINJA WARRIOR OBSTACLE COURSE WITH TEAMS, START A BUSINESS, PLAN A SUPERBOWL OR A NEW YEAR'S EVE PARTY, MAKE HOMEMADE PIZZA AND PLAY A BIG GAME OF FLAG FOOTBALL, MAKE TIE DYE SHIRTS, HAVE A WINTER SLUMBER PARTY AND WATCH ELF, MAKE BUDDY'S FAVORITE BREAKFAST IN THE MORNING (SPAGHETTI TOPPED WITH STRAWBERRY, COCONUT, CHOCOLATE, & RASPBERRY SAUCE, MARSHMALLOWS, AND S'MORE POP-TARTS), MAKE POPSICLES OR HOMEMADE ICE CREAM, HAVE A CAMPOUT, CATCH LIGHTNING BUGS, TELL SCARY STORIES & EAT S'MORES, MAKE FRIENDSHIP BRACELETS, HAVE A WATERMELON SPITTING CONTEST, HAVE A CLOTHES EXCHANGE

WHERE YOU TRADE CLOTHES WITH EACH OTHER THAT DON'T FIT OR YOU NO LONGER WEAR, GO TO A FREE OUTDOOR CONCERT, VISIT A FARMER'S MARKET, BIKE TO DAIRY QUEEN, PLAN POKER NIGHT, LEARN HOW TO BELLY DANCE, PLANT SMALL SUCCULENT POTS OR A GARDEN, MAKE A ZIP LINE, SCHEDULE BOARD GAME NIGHT, HAVE YOUR VERY OWN CHOPPED COMPETITION.

Wayniac shouted out, "Wouldn't texting be considered screen time?"

Mrs. Watson chimed in, "I think what they are trying to say is that you need to take action and invest in healthy relationships and if group texting is one simple way to manage those relationships, that is a solid idea."

"Friends, we are out of time. It is time to go home. We will continue the warm fuzzies into tomorrow. I love this idea and I think that I am going to steal it for years to come."

"Class dismissed; I'll see you on your way out."

One high five after another flew by Mrs. Watson including me in attempt to save her suit jacket from one last concealer splat.

Upon leaving, I launched my backpack over my shoulder and headed down the artwork filled hallway toward mom's classroom. I was hoping to hitch a ride home with her instead of riding the noisy bus.

As I was about to enter my mom's classroom, a distinct voice called out from down the hall, "Wait Maddie!"

I turned towards the voice. Chet walked up to me and sunk a cotton ball into the palm of my hand. My heart melted.

He said, "I really liked working in your group today. Your cotton ball and cold prickly idea saved our grade. See you tomorrow."

All rules are off and since I made them, I can break them. I am NEVER giving up this cotton ball. EVER.

CHAPTER FIVE

Late Bloomer

That night, I tried to find an opportunity to ask Mom when she first got her period. Do I ask between setting the table and taking out the recycling? Do I slide it in at the dinner table? No, definitely not a dinner topic and I didn't want my little sister, Pesty Peyton, asking dumb questions about it. This was difficult enough already without having to deal with her. I really wanted to know, but let's be realistic. *No* time is the right time.

I decided to throw it out there while we were loading the dishwasher after dinner, completely avoiding eye contact, of course.

"Mom, when did you first get your period?"

Mom stopped mid loading of a plate, and twinkly smiled.

"Oh, that's right, you are studying puberty at school. How's that going?"

Was she serious? I was going to have to ask it again? She blew over the question as if I didn't just ask the most embarrassing question of my life. Hello?!

I needed an *exact* age: year, month, and day.

Why do parents make everything hard for kids sometimes?

Being the oldest really has its disadvantages.

If I had an older sister, I'd ask her, and I could avoid this entire conversation altogether. It would be sooooo much easier, but no, I had to be the trailblazer of this family.

Okay, I'll play this 'you are getting older game' with Mom, I decided.

I responded, "We took the puberty test today and we are going over all of the test questions tomorrow. However, Mrs. Watson mentioned that a daughter is likely to have her period around the time that her mother did, and I was curious as to when you first had yours?"

I did it. I threw it out there like it was no big deal. I asked like I was asking what her first car looked like. No biggie.

Sometimes I surprise myself with my maturity and coolthness.

Is that a word? If not, it should be. They could add it to the Webster Dictionary with my picture next to it or look up *coolthness* online and click on images. Bam! My picture would pop up. I'll submit that be added to Webster.com.

"I was kind of a *late bloomer* of sorts," Mom started to say.

My shoulders began caving into the anticipated weight of the rest of the response.

Here comes sucker punch number two.

Are we talking fifteen? Sixteen? Twenty-two?

Roll it out, Mom! T.O.D.A.Y. Can't you see that I am dying to know? I can't be part of the Non-Period Club forever.

"I know it was when I was thirteen. I can't remember if it was the early or late thirteen, but I know your Aunt Cynthia was twelve," Mom continued.

Great. Just great.

Purely fabulous!

Could we be a little vaguer, Mom?

I need more. A LOT more. Like was I exactly twelve years, eleven months, three days, and nine hours.

So, were we talking like one month from now? Twelve months from now? A full sixteen months from now? I prefer to put this on my calendar to prevent any unnecessary surprises.

A little more precise timing is warranted here.

CHAPTER SIX

A Bra "Fitting"

Mom started giving me *that* half smile again. Then she said it. "Maddie, you and I are going to go to the mall this weekend to get fitted for a bra. It's time."

Somebody SAVE ME!

What if someone sees me with *my mom* buying a bra?

What does *fitted* mean anyway? People don't get fitted for underwear. That's considered an undergarment. Why all the hoopla over a bra?

What's the difference? Aren't we talking small, medium, or large size here?

How difficult is that process? Is it necessary to have a full-on bra fitting?

Naaaah. I don't think so. Sounds like a total time waster. Has she actually looked at my chest area?

I asked Mom, "Can't you just pick one up for me when you are out and about?"

"Honey, a lady at the store will need to measure under your arms and around the top of your breasts with a soft tape measure to determine your size. Then the lady will bring in a few different styles to the dressing room to see what fits you best and what you find the most comfortable," Mom oddly excitedly explained.

That sounded completely awful.

A horrific process. How can all of this be necessary?

Mom added, "You should pay attention to any lower back pain which might signify the onset of your period. Also, pay attention to the color of the toilet paper when you wipe to note if you have any red spotting. This will give you a heads up that more may be coming."

Me, "Um, weird, but okay. I will."

Now, I'm going to turn into a complete hypochondriac fretting over these signs on a daily basis. This was all too consuming. Back to my previous plan: Vetoing having my period altogether. I knew it was a good plan from the beginning even though my lower back has had some aching lately. It probably is from when we had yoga class in phy-ed the other day and we had to do all of those impossible yoga moves. I most likely strained my lower back muscles when I was trying to do my *extra* low downward dog yoga move in order to see Chet on the other side of the gym floor past everyone else's mats. You have to do what you have to do. Totally worth it.

Mom being annoyingly giddy suggested, "How about after your bra fitting, we pick up some pads and tampons to have on hand for *the* day it comes?"

I replied with an eye roll, "Sounds fun."

I continued to clean up the kitchen from dinner.

Such an exciting weekend to look forward to.

Welcome to maturity bliss.

Humph.

Ready or not, here come the prison chambers to keep my breasts in on a daily basis, and here's to buying my first *bag* to keep my pads and tampons in.

When did I start being so negative all the time? What has gotten into me? I used to be notoriously known for seeing the sunny side of situations. That's why mom calls me Sunshine. I kinda lost touch with focusing on the positives, keeping it light, and throwing a humorous twist on difficult situations.

Is it part of the hormone changes that happen when people get their period? Am I temporarily cloudy? Will the Sunshine come back?

Is that what PMS is?

I've heard a lot of jokes about it, but I always do the polite fake laugh since I have no idea what any of the jokes actually mean.

Hmmm, PMS…

Period Mean Streak?

That sounds right. I know people talk about feelings of crankiness being common before your period comes. With my mature wit, I didn't really need to listen to all of the questions and answers in the Puberty Question Box after all. Which is good, because I didn't.

Finally, I meandered up to my bedroom to study for my big science test. The next thing I knew, it was morning and my biology book was pasted to my face from my drool. I carefully peeled it off trying to save the page that I needed to memorize for the test. Hopefully, the rule of osmosis is a real thing because if the biology information didn't absorb into my brain overnight, I'm totally doomed.

CHAPTER SEVEN

Virginia, Public & Peanuts

I strolled into Mrs. Watson's class sporting my new denim shorts and flowy pink top looking on point and feeling an overwhelming sense of relief knowing that we were starting a *new* unit that didn't involve anything puberty.

Mrs. Watson announced, "I've decided to switch up the schedule today because I felt the need to bring more attention to and correct some *misinformation* regarding our Puberty Unit."

She has to be joking. Okay, by the look of her poker face, she's not.

This can go one-way or the other. It could either be really interesting or it could be utterly painful. Again.

Mrs. Watson said, "I am writing a few of the answers on the whiteboard that students gave on yesterday's puberty test."

VIRGINIA

PUBLIC

PEANUTS

She turned around with a stoic face and stated, "Nowhere did I teach you anything in this Puberty Unit about the state of *Virginia, public* anything, nor was this a food unit that included *peanuts.* My friends, it is as follows and I will clearly pronounce these words and have you repeat them with me.

VAGINA

PUBIC

PENIS

VIRGINIA is a state located south of Maryland and north of North Carolina.

A **VAGINA** is the passage leading from the uterus to the vulva in females.

PUBLIC is defined as a place open to everyone.

PUBIC refers to the area on your body around either your penis if you are a male or your vulva if you are female, which is not PUBLICly shown.

PEANUTS are a type of nut that grows on a plant.

A **PENIS** is a male organ located by the testicles.

Let's leave the *public* in the state of *Virginia* eating *peanuts* to some future creative writing assignment and focus on proper puberty terminology today."

Hysterical laughter exploded. Me included until…

Wait, was that *my* test she was referring to?

Yikes.

She wouldn't possibly call me out on this in front of everybody, would she?

Being a part of the Non-Period Club and then made out to be the class dork would make this the doubly worst week ever.

Mrs. Watson stated with a boom, "After receiving numerous emails from parents, I felt compelled to explain to you first, why I chose to keep the boys and girls together for this unit. Friends, there is enough mystery surrounding the topic of puberty as far as when is it going to happen, and for some of you wondering why it hasn't happened yet, and others wondering why it has already happened to them." She continued, "I wanted to eliminate as much mystery as I could in order to relieve any potential stress that you may have. I know that complete elimination of puberty stress is virtually impossible but educating all of you inclusively should have eliminated some of the mystery."

Love her for that.

Now, if only she could pass out Post-it Notes with our exact period dates on them, then she'd be a true miracle worker.

Mrs. Watson continued, "*Knowledge* comes from understanding the facts about puberty, but my friends, *wisdom* comes from experience, and *intelligence* is having the ability to adjust to the changes involved with the experience or in this case, puberty."

She walked around the room and continued with her life lesson. "Boys, yes, you will go through voice changes--some squeaks and deep pitches all in one sentence. You'll have hair growth in your armpits, face, and PUBIC area. You may even experience a wet dream, but you will also most likely experience living with a female at some point in your life who will go through puberty. Who knows, you may even be asked to buy your mother, sister, or future wife some pads or tampons while you are grabbing some milk and bread at the store."

Gasps, choking, and gagging sounds filled the room.

The boys were as white as ghosts mortified at the thought of such a barbaric task. The boys chanted statements of refusal.

"Gross!"

"What? No way! Never."

"You couldn't pay me a million dollars to do that!"

Mrs. Watson continued, "This, my friends, is what we call life. You don't get to choose whether or not you go through puberty, just like you don't get to pick your eye color. However, you do get to pick how you deal with it. Either way, you are headed right through the middle. There aren't any shortcuts or free passes. It's not weird. It is what it is. Look to your right. Look to your left. Everyone you see is dealing with it or will deal with it. NBD."

Titan raised his hand and asked, "What is NBD? Is it like PMS, but for boys? Does it mean **N**ever **B**uying **D**eodorant?"

The class burst out with a collective stress-relieving belly laugh.

Mrs. Watson smiled and said with a wink, "No Big Deal."

She cleared the whiteboard and wrote at the top:

Things that I learned about puberty

"My highly intelligent students, please take out a piece of paper. I would like those of you with more experience in this department to write with *wisdom* and I would like those of you who haven't *yet* experienced it personally, to write with *knowledge."*

"What if I don't have either of those two things, Mrs. Watson?" asked Wayniac.

"Wayne, you are a wealth of knowledge and this met with your wit and wisdom should produce some well written puberty lessons. I am more than happy to help you get started if you would like," replied Mrs. Watson.

"That's is okay, Mrs. Watson. I think that I have it. Believe me, I don't want one on one help with puberty." Wayniac said and the class chuckled.

Mrs. Watson walked around the room with a basket and collected all the sheets including Wayne's. Then she walked to the front of the room, rested the basket by her computer, and said, "I encourage all of you to watch for an email this weekend because I will compile an invaluable puberty guide for each of you to keep and refer to as needed."

That is kinda odd and cool at the same time. It might end up being my lifeline someday. One thing that I do know for sure is that I will definitely be checking my computer diligently all weekend for the "*Things that I learned about puberty*" email from Mrs. Watson.

CHAPTER EIGHT

Puke Is a Color Choice?

At home, Mom and I were getting ready to head out for our bra fitting day when Glamma burst through the front door with cinnamon crunch bagels and a gift bag.

"Good Morning my most favorite people on earth!" she sang.

"Hi Glamma. What's the occasion with the gift bag, Glam?" I asked her.

Glamma handed me the pink-and-white, polka dotted bag with a yellow curly-cue ribbon tied to the handle, and told me, "It's for you, Maddie. Open it."

"Really, it's for me?"

I think about today's date, May 15-- just another average day. Strange.

Glamma, erupting with excitement stated, "Yes! Go ahead and open it."

I untied the ribbon and dug curiously through the hot pink tissue and grabbed not one, but two bedazzled zippered pencil-case looking bags.

"Oh thanks, Glamma." I stood up and kissed her.

She gave me her pouty face and said, "You don't like them do you? I can change the jewels to a different color if you'd like."

"I love them. It's just that school is almost out, but I can always use a pencil bag."

Mom and Glamma roared with laughter. "Oh, sweet honey buns, they are *bags* for your pads and tampons," Glamma said, "One for here and one to keep at your dad's house. You know, PADS AT DAD'S!" She died with laughter at her own joke. "At least you will be stylin' with these bling-bling bags, my sweet Maddie!"

Pads at Dad's. Really? Aaaaggghhhh! It never occurred to me that I would have to deal with this at Dad's house. This is an entirely new level of stress that I hadn't even thought about. Can't I arrange for this *period* to only visit when I'm at

Mom's house because she gets these girl things? But Dad? There is absolutely no way that am I doing this period thing at Dad's house.

Glamma added, "I have a few tips that I'll share with you later to help you through your periods."

"Great, I can hardly wait, Glamma." I replied with a very fake smile.

Mom and I slipped out to the mall while Peyton and Glamma did their thing-- whatever that was.

Mom acted all happy-camper-ish as she drove us towards the mall cranking up her funky music and singing unusually loud. Then she reached for the radio dial, turned it down and said, "Sunshine, we are going to start at JCPenney's."

"JCPenney's?" I flatly responded as she pulled into a parking spot.

I obediently trailed behind her, wishing we could just order a bra online and wrap up this "date." I couldn't possibly dread this process anymore. Why on earth am I buying my bras at the same store where I'm certain Great Aunt Tootie buys hers? Great Aunt Tootie has always been a little fruity and I'm not looking to carry that gene on in any way.

Why aren't we at that cute pink store with the pink velvet chairs, where they blast my kind of music throughout the store of cuteness, instead of this 1900's elevator music? Why aren't we at the place that smells hip and fresh, instead of a place that smells like a combination of dog toots and wet socks?

Why not the place where you get a free cute water bottle with your purchase that you can proudly put on your desk at school that shows you're a Period Club member? Hello.

Why can't we be at a place where there is at least ONE shopper under the age of seventy?

Mom couldn't make my life any harder if she tried. I swear she has lost all touch with what it's really like being a tween. I always thought she was a little hipper than my friend's moms. After all, she doesn't wear those awful mom jeans up to her armpits, she is pretty fit, and she's not militant like other moms about bedtime or daily household chores.

Boy, was I wrong when it comes to what being hip *really* means.

Just when I thought JCPenney was bad enough, Mom bounced around a corner to the lingerie department and announced to basically the ENTIRE store, "This is a special day for my daughter and me. We are here for her first bra fitting."

"MOM! Really? They probably have a public announcement speaker system that goes through the *entire* mall if you want to use that instead." I wincingly replied as I'm about to dive under the pajama clothes rack.

"Maddie, there is nothing to be embarrassed about. Every woman goes through several bra fittings in their lifetime." Mom assured me.

"I'm sure when they do it, that they are not on public display, especially at the age of twelve," I mumbled.

"What did you say, honey?" Mom asked.

"Never mind," I said. "Let's just get this painful process over with as soon as possible and can we *please* stay off the bra radar?"

Just then, the store clerk turned towards me with a soft measuring tape draped around her neck as if it's some kind of Heisman Trophy. She stepped back as if to get a good look at me and said, "Oh, hi Maddie. I'm Chet's mom. I believe he's in your class."

Are.You.Serious?

Chet, the most handsome, smart, athletic, hunk-of-muffin boy? THE hottest guy on the face of the universe's mom is going to measure me? What are the odds? How do I get out of this? More importantly, how do I get myself into these situations in the first place?

Chet's mom asked, "So what kind of bra are you looking for?"

Before I could answer, she rattled off, "Are you looking for a push-up bra, padded bra, sports bra, plunge bra, wired bra, wireless bra, bandeau, T-shirt bra, strapless bra…" blah, blah, blah.

Then she continued to name the different colors, "We have fuchsia, black, rose, periwinkle, whipped papaya, salmon, chartreuse, orchid, copper, cobalt, striped, floral…" And then came the fabric list "…Lace, sateen, cotton, damask, denim, silk…"

Mom sensed that my head was spinning out of control, so she threw her hand up and said, "Thank you for your help, but I think Maddie is getting a bit overwhelmed with all of the options. Can we just have her measured and then find a well-fitted sports bra?"

Whew! I'm not exactly sure what a sports bra is, but let's grab one and get out of here. Let's keep the social damage to a minimum.

We proceeded into a large dressing room area. I reluctantly lifted my arms simply mortified to have the hottest guy in my class's mom lay the tape measure across my chest-- or soon-to-be chest.

"Do you have any plans for this summer?" Chet's mom asked.

Who makes small talk at a moment like this? Um, nobody. How can I possibly think about summer plans? All the oxygen is being sucked out of the room and I'm going to faint at any moment. Summer plans?

"Not really," I finally said.

"Chet was thinking about having an end of school party at our house. You should come over. It will be fun," she offered.

Did she just say *Chet, party, and her house* or am I hearing strange things because I can't think clearly when his mom is reaching under both of my armpits with a soft yellowed measuring tape?

She adjusted the tape measure, squinted her eyes, and reached for her tortoise colored reading glasses on top of her head. Finally, she announced proudly, "Let's try a 32A and see how that fits."

Lovely, just lovely.

Good times.

Good times.

I stepped into the dressing room by myself with three boring looking sports bras. I don't remember puke being one of the colors that she listed off. I tried on all three, but there was only one that didn't feel like someone had a belt around my upper rib cage and was cinching down on it as hard as they possibly could, sucking every last bit of air out of me.

Geeez! Women actually wear these prison chambers all day, every day and they pay money for them? *Why* do they do this?

I came out of the dust bunny filled dressing room and proclaimed, "Phew, Done! I'm going to go with this one, but I was wondering if it comes in other colors?"

"I'd be happy to show you what we have. Come this way," she replied.

Chet's mom proudly marched me by bras that looked like the cup sizes of a two-person hammock until we finally came to a small rack where there were two, yes, only two color choices.

I threw my eyebrows up, breathed deeply, and held it in, trying to imagine myself having to debut one of these in the fall in the girls' locker room when we switch into our swimsuits for PE. I just couldn't do it.

I may have to go commando and let them be free. Wait, is commando when you go without underwear or is it without a bra? That was probably in the Puberty Question Box too.

With an extra-long exhale, I asked my mom, "Do you think maybe we can keep looking?"

Chet's mom quickly excused herself to help another customer.

Mom looked down at me and quietly said, "Honey, I only came here to get you measured and if by chance, you saw something that you liked, we'd pick it up. I wanted you to feel more comfortable and confident when we went to Victoria's Secret to get something more age appropriate."

I KNEW SHE WAS COOL!

CHAPTER NINE

WARNING: Bra Hazard Ahead

Why did I doubt her? She had a smooth plan all along. She always does.

Yes! I knew I was going to be able to change in gym class without wanting to hide in the bathroom stall. What a BIG relief! I love her.

We slid out of JCPenney's and headed down the mall corridor.

Mom started digging in her purse. I didn't ask any questions.

We just kept moving in the direction of the cool bra and panty store with its tall pink velvet chairs.

"We are finally here," Mom said as we entered an entirely different time zone. It was two whole worlds away from the last bra place. Maybe this isn't going to be so bad after all. Then again, I'm pretty sure I could have this feeling anywhere but where Great Aunt Tootie buys her bras. Who knows, maybe it *was* the relief of already having the dreaded fitting done? Who knows and who really cares, at this point?

I blew through the store like I owned it. A longhaired beautiful blonde girl with a soft pink measuring tape around her neck approached me and said, “Can I help you find something?”

I confidently announced, “Yes, please. I am looking for a fun bra that doesn’t have a bunch of stuffing in it.”

Oh no! I think they call it padding? I’m blew my cover in less than two seconds. Reel it in, Maddie, reel it in. You’ve got this…

I saved face and said, “Well, what I meant was that I’m looking for an everyday bra.” She swished her long locks behind her shoulder and whisked us to the back of the store past mannequins with bedazzled bras and panties. No question, this is definitely where Glamma shops.

Then there, in front of me, were a mass variety of bras in different colors and shapes. It was as if we were in a taffy factory with a zillion colored flavors strewn from one end of the wall to the other.

Mom supportively hung back just enough as my eyes rolled back and forth across the panoramic array of vibrant colors. The young store assistant asked, "Do you know your bra size, or would you like to get measured today?"

I told her my size as if I'd known my entire life, like it was my middle name.

"32A." I said proudly.

I picked out six different colors and headed into the pink, queen-like dressing room with gold accents everywhere. Upon entering, I noticed that they had the word ***DIVA*** written in pure gold letters across my dressing room door. There is no doubt that it was real gold, but how did they know my name?

A coincidence?

I think not.

I was meant for this place.

They've probably been holding this room for me my *entire* life.

I didn't even notice, but I probably have a designated parking spot outside in front of the store with, yet another personalized gold **DIVA** sign staked at the front of it.

I locked my door, took off my shirt, looked in the mirror and said quietly, "Well, here it goes." I grabbed the hot pink bra off of the velvet hanger, and I put my hands above my head to slip it on like a T-shirt or a sports bra.

Like any *professional* would.

In no time, I was so tangled in the straps and bands and cuppy things that the only way out of this messed-up web of straps and silky cups was to cut it off of me.

And I thought this was going SO smoothly.

The struggle was real.

I was *trapped.*

A REAL LIFE BOOBY TRAP.

"Ummmmmmmm, Mom!"

She knocked because she couldn't get in my locked dressing room.

I was contorted in this bra. I couldn't figure out how to finagle low enough to bend and unlock the door.

I'm finished. Done for.

The headlines will read,

Death by Strangulation of Bra in Her Personal Diva Dressing Room.

Fabulous, just fabulous.

Nice grand finale, Maddie!

Mom calmly asked, "Honey, unlock the door please."

Daaah! *I'm trying!*

I have no choice but to tell her, "Mom, this is SERIOUS. You will need to *hit the deck* and crawl *under* the dressing room door ASAP."

Mom, being the logical one, searched for a fitting room attendant to let her in, but you'd swear the fire alarm went off and everyone fled the store because there was *no one* to be found *anywhere,* as I'm slowly losing consciousness.

Mom, being the most awesome mom on earth, threw her purse under the door and did the full-on army crawl, belly dragging on the floor and all. She popped up to her feet once her bum cleared the door like a superhero.

Super Mom sprung up and as she was about to ask me what the problem was, she burst out laughing. Tears streamed down her cheeks and she suddenly crossed her legs like she was going to pee her pants or something because she simply couldn't contain herself.

Okaaaaayyyyy, superhero status wiped clean.

She finally collected herself and said, "Oh, Maddie, what on earth happened?"

"Mom! Do something before all of my circulation is gone. I'm near death here!" I yelled frantically.

"Turn around," mom quickly replied as she turned my shoulders.

She unhooked something and it was like letting one side of a tug-of-war rope go after each side was pulling with all their might. The straps whipped around my head and chest at deadly speed.

My girls were *free* at last!

I barely escaped death. "Why don't these bra contraptions come with directions?

Hello! This *isn't* an innate thing." I exclaimed.

Mom finally recovered after wiping her drenched face. Nice. Glad *someone's* enjoyed themselves.

"Mom, I'm sure we can order these bras online and skip all this drama Let's get out of here. I'm over this. Please?" I begged her.

Mom ignored me and proceeded to show me three sets of hooks on the back that you first unhook, then turn upside down with the cups hanging in a reverse triangle way with the hooks draping in the front. Then you latch the two middle hooks together, sashay it around until the hooks are about to the center or your back and the reverse triangles are on your belly, and grab the two straps, sticking one arm into the center of each strap and pulling up over your shoulders and adjusting until comfortable.

"No problem, Mom. One hundred and seventy-two steps. I'm sure I've got it." I sharply replied.

It's likely that I will get caught in *another* webbed mess prior to mastery of the bra.

"Okay, now you try it without my help," Mom said.

The teacher in her can't be removed from any situation.

I awkwardly accomplished the task with an enormous amount of patience from both of us.

Feeling slightly more mature, I finally told her, "I'm good now."

Meaning Mom, Step out NOW. Bye.

"Now, I would like you to try a bra that has the hook in the front," she said, instead of leaving.

"More options?" I sputtered, "Is this *necessary*? Today? Haven't I gone through enough already?"

Mom proceeded to explain that some women prefer the front hook.

"They find it more comfortable," she said convincingly.

Comfortable and bras aren't interchangeable words, for starters. I rolled my eyes and reluctantly answered with a slow moan, "I guess I'll try it because I am never going through this bra fitting marathon process *EVER* again."

Mom disappeared forever on a hook-in-the-front bra hunt. I rested in my personalized dressing room, thinking about what the store clerk said when she was showing me the wall of colored bras. I've got it! She waved her arm and said something about nude bras.

Brilliant! I will just go with the *nude* concept. Nude means nude, right? Then *nude* means no bra. Perfect! Sign me up for the nude plan. Why wasn't this presented to me from the beginning? Not wearing anything means I won't have anything lacy or hot pink to put on in the locker room, but who cares when *nude* is acceptable? I'm sure that the store clerk who works at a bra store knows best. Dah! She was the one who mentioned it anyway. I feel so much better now. What a relief!

Mom returned and knocked on the door. "Maddie, open the door, I have some new bras for you to try on."

I opened the door fully dressed and she gave me a weird look and said, "Why are you dressed?"

"Mom, I've decided to go with *nude.*" I cleverly responded.

"Okay, honey, but we still need to pick a style whether it be a hook-in-the-front bra or the hook-in-the-back kind. Then you can pick any color you want."

"I said that I picked nuuuuude. Now, please, let's get out of here."

Here we go again, but this time it was even worse. Mom laughed so hard that she was wiping both her eyes and her nose. Really? This is definitely the most mentally draining experience that I have ever had.

Mom finally explained, "N*ude* is a color choice for a bra color. Women sometimes choose to wear it when they wear light-colored tops to conceal the bra so it isn't as noticeable."

"Oh, right." I respond flatly.

I surrendered to trying on the bras that she had strung over her arm--with her help, of course.

Then she said, "Maddie, I have some coupons in my purse for a free beach bag and water bottle with a bra purchase if you want to use them?"

"Yes, SCORE! Of course, I want to use them."

I picked out *two* bras. No boring nude ones. If I had to wear these things, they might as well be stylish for my locker room reveal.

The clerk wrapped each of them in striped pink tissue paper and placed them in an extra-large pink bag with elaborate cloth handles.

The smiley cashier dropped in a free awesome pink beach bag and a stellar pink water bottle.

This is going to be the best summer ever.

CHAPTER TEN

The Unannounced *Friend*

Maybe getting older will be okay.

I definitely aged five years through my bra strangulation experience.

There really should be *strangulation warnings* on all bra tags and warning signs on the dressing room doors: *May cause bodily harm or even result in death.*

Just sayin', it could save a life. My steps were lighter and the puberty cloud seemed to fade as we walked through the mall.

"Do you want to grab something to eat in the food court?" Mom asked.

"Sure," I maturely replied.

I carried *the* pink striped bag thinking *maybe* somebody would see me and think I'm in the Period Club now. Chances are high on a rainy

Saturday at the mall that I'll bump into somebody.

Mom and I decided to treat ourselves and eat at Potbelly's. She gave me her food order and some cash while I stood in Potbelly's line as she headed to the restroom.

And what do you know? Mia, Brianna, and Lily, all members of the Period Club, came up from behind me. "Hi Maddie," they said in unison.

"Hi, what's up?" I asked.

I threw my shopping bag over my shoulder owning all the glory of the pink striped bag.

"Not much," they replied as the worker asked for my order.

"Two grilled chicken and cheddar sandwiches, two bags of dill pickle chips, and two fountain drinks please." I ordered.

I was secretly distracted by hearing their partial comments as I was providing the clerk our order.

"Oh, my gosh!"

"Do you think she has any idea?"

"You tell her."

"No, you tell her."

I paid and slid down the line to stand under the Order Pick Up arrow.

A pink striped bag doesn't do much for me when I look like a complete loser appearing to be at the mall alone and ordering enough food to feed an NFL player.

Personally, I think it's most productive to shop alone because then you aren't waiting for other shoppers to be done and also you don't have to go into stores that you have no interest in. But for some unspoken teen social rule, it's just *not cool* to shop at the mall *alone*. Ever.

I hesitantly glanced down the counter and saw all three of them staring at me with wide eyes. I shot back a weak smile.

"Order 113" a burly voice bellowed. Thank goodness. That's our order. I showed the man my receipt, grabbed the tray, and turned to bolt to a table.

I felt a gentle hand on my back and then two arms wrapping something around my waste. I turned and it was Brianna, Mia, and Lily.

Brianna said, "Maddie, I think that your 'friend' has officially arrived."

"Friend?" I ignorantly responded as Lily finished tying a jacket around my waste. Is that some sort of slam because I appeared to be a total *loner* at the moment?

I was completely clueless as to what Brianna was referring to when she said "friend."

Lily winked at me and very softly said, "Let's go to the bathroom, new club member."

What?! *That* friend? Right here in the middle of the mall food court? With WHITE shorts on? This *can't* be happening. Purely, mortified. Sweat covered my body. I almost dropped the tray of food, but to my surprise, Mom grabbed it as I turned toward the restroom.

Mom joyfully said, "Hi girls. What a nice surprise to see you three!"

Suddenly, she noticed a weirdness in the air and quickly asked me, "Do you want to pick a seat to sit down and eat, Maddie?"

"Mom, I'll be right back. I have to run to the restroom quickly with Lily."

I ran like a racehorse coming out of the gates at the Kentucky Derby straight to the nearest restroom.

Lily followed closely behind and then led us into the large handicap bathroom stall. She pulled out her period bag and handed it to me.

"Take the pad out of here and put the sticky side down on your panties and then stick the smaller sides around the bottom of your panties for extra security." Lily explained and stepped out of the stall.

I fumbled through it by doing exactly as instructed and met her at the sink to wash my hands.

Lily leaning against the wall said, "You can keep my coat wrapped around your waste to hide the back side of your shorts and just bring it to me at school on Monday."

Overwhelmed by her kindness and the hard fact that I am having my period, I fell awkwardly silent.

As I grabbed for the paper towels, I finally broke my silence, "You are the sweetest. Thank you for helping me and for loaning me your jacket. I will wash it and give it back to you on Monday. How can I ever repay you?"

"I've been in your shoes. Just pay it forward new PC member," she said with a warm smile as she disappeared out of the restroom.

In somewhat of a fog, I walked through the food court to find Mom, thinking what a sweeter world this would be if we all paid it forward and how sometimes I make things up in my head that aren't really happening at all. The girls weren't being mean. They were trying to figure out if I was aware of my short situation and which one of them was going to approach me about it without embarrassing me. I'm my own worst enemy sometimes. I need to get back to my old sunshine self, thinking the best of people.

By now, I'm standing next to Mom at our table.

"Is everything alright?" Mom asked.

I responded, "Yes, but I think we need to expedite filling the bedazzled bags that Glamma gave me this morning. And I hope you can work some magic on getting a red stain out of these white shorts." Her eyes bugged out of her head. "Okay then, let's eat and go to Target before we head home. And Sunshine, can you please remind me to pick up some dark chocolates when we are there?"

Is this something else that I'm supposed to know too? What does chocolate and stained shorts have to do with one another? Where's the puberty manual? Why hasn't somebody thought of this? It would be a bestseller. A lifeline of sorts.

A Puberty Survival Guide

How to Survive Puberty

The Club's Secret Handbook

"Maddie, this seems like a good time to tell you about my puberty story. It's not exactly a proud moment, but things were different when I was a kid."

Even though I was obsessed with getting home to see if Mrs. Watson's email of puberty lessons hit my email yet, I was equally curious to hear mom's puberty story.

"Puberty was not talked about at home. I think parents thought the schools handled it. Well, not so much. I was on my own in that department. I was around your age when I noticed a lot of my friends had bras and cool underwear when we changed in gym class one day. I had granny gruns as we called them back in-the-day. They were full coverage underwear with cheap elastic waistbands and you spent half the day yanking them up to your armpits in order to keep them on. Not to mention, I didn't even own a bra then."

Mom reached for her napkin and continued, "I figured, a girl has to do what a girl has to do. So, I rummaged through my drawers and decided the closest thing I had to a bra was my swimsuit top. I thought I had solved the problem for the time being. I wore it to school the next day and someone asked me if I had swimming lessons after school since they noticed the tied straps of the suit top dangling out of the back of my shirt collar."

"Oh my gosh," I giggled.

Mom continued, "Well, then that day after school, I took matters into my own hands and I gathered up my birthday money and headed down to Walmart on my stars and stripes banana seat bike with red and blue pom-pom handlebars."

I can see mom now racing down the street with pigtails and that determined look she gets.

"Completely unaware that bras had sizes and panicking that I might see someone I knew; I grabbed a big pink lace bra and matching non-granny like panties. I checked out, biked home, ran straight to my room, and slipped them on. The bra looked Dolly Parton HUGE on me!"

"Who is Dolly Parton?" I asked.

Mom replied, "A former petite country music singer with an unusually large chest."

I started to laugh imagining my mom trying to navigate this monstrosity.

"I couldn't possibly get myself to take it back and exchange it. So, I took the last two rolls of toilet paper out of our only bathroom and I tucked the perforated sheets into each side of my bra. I filled them up, stretched my shirt over them, and walked downstairs. My parents looked at me oddly as if I was working on a Dolly Parton Halloween costume or something. Your Uncle Todd, rounded the corner and with big eyes said, 'Mom, what happened to Molly?'"

"Uncle Todd's comment sent me running straight out of the front door and down the street to Shannon's house. She was impressed with my creativity and I decided that's all that mattered. If Shannon thought I was fine, I was set for school."

"Mom! You actually went to school with those on? OMG." I asked inquisitively.

Mom laughingly added, "Oh, that's not even the worst of it. The next day in class, Nick leaned over and asked me if he could borrow some toilet paper for his bloody nose. Apparently, under my armpit of my sleeveless shirt, it looked like the tail end of the toilet paper roll. Which it was, but I didn't realize everyone thought I had a classroom supply!"

"MOM! I'm dying!"

"It gets worse, a few days later, I got my period for the first time and woke up with red PJ bottoms and stained sheets. At first, I wasn't even certain what happened, but when I figured it out, I panicked. I ripped off all my sheets, took off my PJ's, and threw everything into the washing machine. I did what any sensible person would do, I tripled the detergent to ensure *all* the blood stains would come out."

"Then what?"

"Well, I ran back upstairs and jumped in the shower. When I turned the water off, I heard a knock at my bathroom door."

"Who was it?"

"By the four knocks, pause, two knocks, I knew it was Glamma. I wrapped myself with a towel and opened the door to find her standing in the doorway with her bedazzled snorkel goggles and pink glitter diving fins on. Glamma was trying to speak through her snorkel breathing tube. As if I could understand what shenanigans she was up to at the moment."

"I can see Glamma rocking out the glitzy snorkel gear. LOL," I commented.

"Long story short, she came to tell me that the laundry room mysteriously flooded with bubbles. Yup, that's my story," Mom said as she nodded her head, perked up her eyebrows, and rolled her lips into her mouth.

She continued, "I had many erratic and unpredictable teenage years. Many days were filled with obsessing over things that really didn't matter. Some days, I battled trying to keep my three-inch bangs hiked on top of my head with endless cans of Aqua Net hairspray. Other days, I obsessed with digging out stuck food from my buck teeth hidden behind my dismal gray braces. I often fretted about acne and my unpredictable timing of my period. The one hundred and one silly things I worried about through puberty that no one noticed, but me."

She paused, looked across the food court and then looked directly into my eyes, "Sunshine, some of the hardest parts during those years were dealing with peer pressure and trying to figure out the constantly shifting set of social hierarchy that seemed to almost change overnight in school. Believe me, I truly loved those years, but it still was, at times, a treacherous passage. I want you to know that you can come to me and ask me anything. I won't judge. I am here to help you navigate through and enjoy the ride as best you can. These years can be your best years. I love you, Sunshine." Mom reached for my hand.

"I love you too, mom. I am actually happy to hear that you had some challenges. For some weird reason, I always think that because you had Glamma, things had to be a little cooky, but open and easy."

Mom glanced at her watch. "Definitely cooky, but not always a walk in the park. We better get to Target. It's later than I thought."

If Target wasn't an absolute necessity right now, I'd beg mom to boogie home so I could check for the lifeline and print off the much-needed puberty instruction book. But the Target run is classified as a *need*, not a want, in my life right now. I'm not looking to attempt doing my first load of laundry in the morning. Especially with Glamma in the house.

CHAPTER ELEVEN

Perfumed Tampons & Pads That Fly

My appetite went to zero after this charade. So, I pushed my food around on my plate until mom finished. Thankfully, she didn't ride me about not eating. We threw our food in the trashcan and took off for Target.

I was pleasantly surprised when on the short drive there mom suggested, "Sunshine, how about sometime next week, we make a quick run to the mall to see if we can find you a cute outfit to wear to Chet's end-of-the-year party?"

"That would be awesome!" I responded shockingly. Since my parent's divorce, shopping has been cut to a minimum even with mom doing some extra tutoring on the side. So, this is an extra special cool mom move.

At Target, my head swiveled around three hundred sixty degrees like an owl the *entire* time we were in the sanitary napkin aisle. I stood in front of a sea of pads trying my hardest to focus, grab, and go. Who knew there were so many to pick from? There were ones with *wings*. Why wings? Do they actually fly? Or was the one Lily had given me with the fold over edges a *winged* one? Probs.

There were ones so "thick" they looked like diapers. OMG, I'd look like a penguin trying to waddle around with that stuck between my legs.

Whoa! *Deodorant* pads? Why would I set myself up for that? Wouldn't everyone know *that* deodorant smell and know you have a pad on?

Hmmm, *thin* ones. What is the point beyond a guaranteed red stained white short problem?

Mom walked between the shelf and me. "Maddie, let's start with the medium size and the thin ones because in the beginning your period will be light and spotty. We can get different ones when we need to." Mom explained.

"Alright." I agreed in order to make a quick exit stage left of this aisle.

Mom pointed to the opposite side of the aisle and pointed to all of the tampons and said, "Sunshine, grab one box."

Again, the labels were mystifying. "Sporty" popped out at me. "Sporty'? How can a tampon possibly be "sporty?" Okay….no clue on this side either.

"Mom, please grab one and let's get out of here. You said this would be quick."

Thankfully, she refrained from another one of her teaching moments for another time and grabbed a box that said Tampax on it. She also grabbed a bag of dark chocolate Dove candies on the way to the checkout counter. I maintained my three hundred sixty-degree maneuver at the checkout line to ensure no one saw our two boxes of sanitary pads, one box of tampons, and the Dove chocolates.

Still clueless as to why we had to buy the chocolates, but at this point, I don't care enough to ask.

The Target clerk asked mom, "Did you know that it is buy one box of Tampax, get one free this week?"

Mom, "No, I didn't."

Target clerk, "Would you like another box?"

Mom, "Of course, if it is free. We can always use them."

The Target clerk turned on her red ambulance flashing light above the cash register indicating the line is being held up and proceeded to get on her walkie talkie. She had the volume set at maximum decibels possible and asked, "Could someone please bring me a box of Tampax tampons to Checkout Lane 21?"

I am about ready to hit the deck. WHO DOES THAT?

This is so EXTRA.

I glanced at mom. She's happy as a lark knowing she is scoring a free box of tampons. OMG! Get me out of here and SHUT OFF THAT FLASHING LIGHT!

A handsome, athletic, high school age boy handed me the dreaded free box as I stood frozen in the checkout lane. He locked eyes with me and smiled. "Are these the correct ones?" he asked.

Oddly, he looks like an older version of Chet.

Mom sees me frozen, grabbed the box, and replied, "Yes, thank you Mr. Johnson." She handed them to the cashier and the boy disappeared as fast as he came.

Did she just say *Johnson*? Could this be an older brother? I adjusted the jacket around my waist to ensure full coverage.

Mom at glacial speed completed the transaction.

"Thank you for the free box." Mom said with a warm smile to the cashier.

I grabbed the bag and briskly walked with the longest stride possible to get out of the store. I muted myself because mute is better than diarrhea-ing endless negative comments to mom right now. I know she's trying and this is *special* to her. I love her, but the *special* date is beyond over as far as I'm concerned.

This is officially the loooongest day ever recorded.

On the way home, my stomach was growling louder than the radio station. Mom must have heard it because she called Glamma on the car phone to check in about dinner plans.

"Hi Mom, I wanted to see if Maddie and I could pick you and Peyton up and go out to dinner?" Mom asked.

"That would be simply FABULOUS! I will put my lips on and find my bling-bling purse. No worries, Peyton and I will be ready lickety-split." Glamma's reply filled the car and she hung up.

Ugh. That is the LAST thing that I want to do. I would rather starve to death and stay home to read my email from Mrs. Watson than go out-to-eat putting off getting the info on puberty. I need it now more than ever. But how can I possibly skip out on dinner after Mom spent the entire day helping me figure out this bra thing and she saved my life in the process?

I decided to hold my tongue. Again.

Once we got home, I made a mad-dash up the stairs with the Victoria Secret and Target bags. I immediately changed my shorts and panties and wandered into the bathroom, locked the door, and broke open the medium size pad box. I read the directions and followed the diagram step by step on the paper insert that was inside of the box. I washed my hands and went back into my room. Finally, I threw open my laptop and logged in to check my school email. *BAM!* There it was, a school email from the one and only, Mrs. Watson.

I clicked on it; my heart pounded loudly. I immediately noticed the list contained much more than twenty-eight puberty lessons.

It had fifty-three! Holy moly, fifty-three. Interesting….

Mrs. Watson's short intro stated that she decided to include all the slips that were put into the "Puberty Question Box" throughout the unit, including the ones she found in the box after the test.

Hmmm… I didn't think of putting some in *after* the test. I was too busy worrying about the Period Club.

Now, onto the *THE LIST*. This should be extra juicy and informative. Woot, woot! Finally, to be in the *know*. Now, I can step away entirely from this grey cloud of puberty cluelessness without the fear of looking like a dumb butt. I need to print this off.

"Maddie, we are all starving and waiting for you. How much longer, honey?" Mom yelled upstairs.

Really? I have the key to unlock all the mysteries of my life right here with the click of a button. Who cares about food?

"Maddie?" Mom called again.

"Mom, can I take a rain check and you three go ahead and grab some pizza?" I said cringing as I waited for her reply.

"What? I thought you were so hungry on the way home?" Mom responded.

I'll admit, my stomach was growling loudly on the way home, but what is more important? Food for survival or reading the puberty bible? Daaah!

How do I get rid of these three quickly so I can flop down on the couch and get instructions to teen life? Why do we always have to do everything T-O-G-E-T-H-E-R?

To my complete surprise, Mom yelled up, "No problem, honey. We'll bring you back some pizza."

YESSSSS! Score Big Time!!!!

"Thanks, Mom!" I yelled ecstatically.

"No worries." Mom replied.

Easy for you to say. Well, maybe after I read this, there won't be any more worries. Whew, now that would be a major load off.

I decided to resend it to myself to have another copy just in case I ever accidentally deleted the document. I'm also going to save it to my "Life" folder on my computer. Then I'm printing not one, not two, but *three* copies. Yup, that should secure this little treasure.

I hit "print three copies" and then slid down the stair banister. I've always wanted to try this. A total NO-NO when Mom's home. "You'll break your neck, arm…"

With fireman-going-down-the-pole speed, I stood over the printer and waited for our dinosaur of a printer to kick out the first copy.

It came out of the printer millimeters at a time and then the paper got sucked back into the printer, making a choking sound. Are you serious? *PAPER JAM* flashed across the screen. This stuff only happens to me. Why can't we have a laser printer like all of my friends have?

I pulled out the printer, took off the back panel, and there was my lifeline--all torn, scrunched, wadded up over the wheel that feeds the paper through. I paused and looked at the chewed-up mess. Yup, my puberty life looks a lot like this right now.

BUT being the problem solver that I am, and seeing this as only a small obstacle, I unplugged it and hacked at it with a butter knife. I tried to get all of the shredded paper ends out of the unit. I slammed the back panel on, plugged it in, pressed OK on the screen panel, and sprinted back upstairs leaping ten steps at a time. I hit print again, and slid back downstairs, fireman style.

At this point, I prayed for this stupid, archaic machine to cough out at least one complete set of Mrs. Watson's life lessons. I stood over it with my thumb and pointer finger holding onto the page as if I could make it come out faster.

BAM! One complete set. I jumped over the back of the couch, plopped down, and absorbed E.V.E.R.Y. last word on this list.

CHAPTER TWELVE

Unsolved Mysteries Solved

*Not everyone goes through puberty between ages twelve and fourteen. Late bloomers are just as normal as early bloomers.

~Um, not helpful at all.

*Headaches can happen when you have your period. Try exercising and sometimes eating chocolate, which has caffeine in it, both can help.

~Ohhh, Dove chocolates from Target. Got it. Check.

*Acne is part of puberty. Keep your hands off of your face, especially when you are sitting. Don't support your head with your hand on your chin. Your hands are full of dirt and bacteria, which transfers to your pores and can give you acne.

~But how do I stay awake in class then? Great this is one more thing to add to my germaphobe list.

*Girls should always wipe from front to back to avoid UTIs (Urinary Tract Infections) UTIs can be painful.

~Great! I've been in reverse for eleven-plus years! Good to know NOW!

*Sex and intercourse can mean the same thing.

~Daaah!

*Wash your face in the morning and in the evening with a mild cleanser or plain soap and water to remove dirt. Also, wash your pillowcase once a week to keep acne at bay.

~This is doable.

*If you have dry skin, moisturize with an unscented and an alcohol-free cream after washing. If you have oily skin, use an over the counter cleansing pad containing salicylic acid, benzoyl peroxide, or one that has sulfur in it.

~How do I know if I have oily or dry skin?

*Acne is strongly genetic. Maintain healthy skincare, but no matter how hard you work to keep on top of this, know that it isn't all in your control.

~I need to ask mom and dad about their teen acne ASAP.

*Never pop pimples. It increases your risk of infection and scarring.

~Woah, scarring?

*Shower EVERY single day.

~Eye roll

*School nurses have an ample supply of pads and tampons if you need them.

~And if it's a male nurse…then what?

*The monthly period cycle is irregular (which means, not monthly) for the first few years.

~How is this helpful?!

*A virgin is someone who has never had sexual intercourse (and it's not the same as the state of Virginia!)

~This one stuck permanently in class yesterday. Got it.

*PMS stands for "Premenstrual Syndrome." Sometimes people get irritable prior to the onset of your period. This can be alleviated by proper diet, sleep, and exercise.

~This is lame. Mine is SO much better. Pre-Mean Streak. More definitive.

*Deodorant is a fragrance that masks body odor. Antiperspirants reduces or stops sweat. Sweat alone does not have an odor. When sweat is combined with bacteria, it creates an unpleasant scent oftentimes referred to as BO (Body Odor). Please use according to your body's needs on a *daily* basis. It is a gift to those around you.

~Yaaaa! I hope Zoe Flanhopper sees this one!

*Some kids who go through puberty gain weight, some grow tall, some both, and some neither.

~Basically, worthless info.

*A *penis* is a male sex organ located by the testicles, never to be misspelled or mispronounced with the word *peanuts*.

~NEVER eating peanuts again!

*Growing bigger hips doesn't mean you are gaining weight. You are getting curves.

~Great....

*Always have pads or tampons handy for the first couple of years until you settle into a more regular menstrual schedule.

~ Basically, you are saying to strap on a fanny pack 24/7?

*Stress and lack of sleep can trigger acne outbreaks.

~In bed by 9:00 PM every night going forward.

*Breasts grow at different rates, and most girls won't have symmetrical breasts. More often than not, one will be bigger than the other.

~Especially when one loses circulation upon bra entrapment!

*People aren't all size zero. Magazine covers are photoshopped and air brushed. Nobody looks that good without a lot of computer help. There is no such thing as perfection.

~Can you connect me with some of these photoshop experts to help with my yearbook pic then? Just asking…

*Sore breasts can indicate that your period is coming.

~Hmmmm

*Tampons do not hurt when you insert one, and you can't feel a tampon once it's inserted.

~Nice try to be convincing. Still not interested-- yet.

*An erection is when the penis becomes erect or firm. It's a complexity of vascular, psychological, endocrine, and sometimes it is a sexual arousal, but not always-it can also be a spontaneous event.

~Whew! I can cross that off my worry list.

*Menstrual blood can be bright red to dark brown. All is normal.

~Ewwwwwwwww! Ugh!

*Birth control is a prescription which is sometimes used to regulate periods and it may help with acne. It doesn't mean someone is having intercourse if they are taking birth control.

~ *Didn't know this one....*

*If you do not change you tampon regularly, you can go into toxic shock, which can be life threatening.

~What part of puberty isn't shocking?

*Boys' upper lip hair starts off looking like peach fuzz.

~Hmmm, this explains Chet's new hairy upper lip. Dreamy.

*A boy's penis grows throughout puberty.

~TMI- Too Much Information.

*It's okay to swim when you have your period if you take the right precautions. The easiest one being using a tampon. You won't make the water red, just like peeing in the pool doesn't make the water blue.

~Not buying it. Have you seen the movie Grown Ups? The dad pees in the pool and it turns blue. Just sayin'.

*Some women shave their legs, armpits, arms, and pubic areas. Some only shave their armpits. Some do none of the above. You do you.

~Sounds like a lot of work.

*Your period may last twelve, ten, three, or even two days. It does not always fall under the classic seven days. It's a moving target for the first few years.

~Lovely, just plain lovely. Another moving target.

*Some soaps can irritate your vagina. Try to use a mild soap or body wash and be sure to wash with water to remove all soap. It may feel like a burning sensation if you don't.

~Note to self….

*You will need to change your pad or tampon more frequently on the days when the flow is heavier.

~Daaah, a given.

*Never shave without shaving cream. Let the cream sit for a minute to soften the hair follicles, and never use a dull razor. Doing so can cause razor burn and a nasty rash.

~Dying right now at Luke's blazing red razor-chafed face last week! Who knew?

*It's normal for boys' voices to crack during puberty.

~But on Chet, it's a.d.o.r.a.b.l.e!

*Wet dreams are when you have a sexually arousing dream that occurs during sleep and a male's body releases semen. They are normal for boys. You can't control when it happens, but you can strip the sheets and wash them when it does.

~ Finally, ONE tip that I can cross off.

*Find some sort of exercise that you enjoy and focus on health/fitness rather than size and weight change during puberty.

~Is Netflix a sport?

*You can experience growing pains from growing at such a rapid rate during puberty. It can produce stretch marks, but there is nothing you can do to prevent those. They will fade and they won't be purple/pink forever. Keeping your body moisturized can help.

~If Mom and Glamma are any indication, I have no worries of stretch marks on my breasts, anyway.

*Pubic hair is coarse and curly--and concealed from the Public. It is located in the pubic area.

~Yup, you made this point pretty clear, Mrs. Watson. I'm pretty sure none of us will mispronounce this word ever again.

*It's normal for vaginas to have discharge, and you may have gunk in your panties some days.

Vaginas are self-cleaning and self-lubricating. It can also have different smells at different times of the month. Again, all of this is normal.

~Oh, my GAWD. She actually answered this puberty box question. Weirdorama.

*Teens get moody. It's normal. You might not notice it, but the people around you will.

~Doubt it! I'm always bursting with sunshine. Okay, well I'm working on getting back to that.

*Your DNA helps determine when puberty will start.

~Good times asking your mom about this one. Not.

*Don't flush pads and tampons down toilets. It can clog them. Wrap them in toilet paper and dispose of them in the garbage. Be sure to take the garbage out often. It will start stinking!

~THIS is what Mia did at Lily's birthday party when she was in the bathroom forever and then she came running out as the flood gates opened and the water came out like a tidal wave into the kitchen. I TOTALLY get it now. Hilarious! I'm never flushing these down a toilet. Never pulling a "Mia."

*You don't need to wash your bra daily like you do with your panties--unless you sweat profusely in them.

~Okay, so how often then? Details please.

*STD stands for Sexually Transmitted Disease. This means that an infection is transmitted through sexual contact, caused by bacteria, viruses, or parasites.

~Scary.

*Abstinence is the only 100% way not to become pregnant or be infected with an STD. Abstinence means abstaining from, or not having sexual intercourse.

~Oh, that was the answer that I needed on the test.

*Wash your pubic area and your underarms every single day because perfume and cologne doesn't cover up B.O. (Body Odor). Take a shower every day.

~I hope Jake Hines reads this and tones down the Axe cologne. Save us all!

*Discovering romantic feelings for others is normal. The girl or boy that you have known for years may all of a sudden be cute. These crushes can be intense causing butterflies or heart flutters.

~Pretty sure Chet has been HOT since kindergarten in my book anyway. Forget butterflies with Chet. I feel the whole zoo when I think about him!

*Budding is when your breasts start developing. Get a bra fitting, buy a bra, and wear it.

~Shouldn't this statement come with a HAZARD WARNING or how-to instructions?

*There are many different pads; some are thick, thin, deodorized, and some have wings. Tampons come in different sizes. Some have plastic applicators that you use to insert and then throw away, and there are deodorized options available, too.

~Note to self: Purchase in the OFF hours so you aren't seen in THAT aisle of the store. Also, take note of any coupons or BOGO's going on.

*It's okay to talk to your parents about any of this. They will be relieved that you are asking questions. Sometimes, they just don't know how to bring it up. They have all gone through it.

~Not exactly an easy step, but worth the leap.

Wow, I didn't expect such a solid list. This is quite a gold mine. Some of these tips are new to me and some are just plain basic info, but I'll admit that most of them fall under the category of "good to know" and some of them even fall under the category of 'it might save me from some serious social embarrassment one day.'

CHAPTER THIRTEEN

Maddie-isms

Hmmm…I do need to add to this list though. It requires a few tweaks, some simple Maddie *wisdom* additions.

I headed to the kitchen and whipped up some gorp: goldfish, raisins, cheerios, M&M's, and pretzel sticks. I grabbed my water bottle and headed upstairs to my room for some light editing.

With my snacks handy and my laptop resting on my legs, I reached over and flipped on my radio and sunk back into my comfy, pink fluffy pillows piled on my bed. I started typing.

Oh, this is going to be good. My hands flew over the keyboard as if it had been brewing in me my whole life.

1. Avoid white or even light-ish colored shorts if your period is coming.

2. Taylor Swift, Beyoncé, Sam Smith, Kim Kardashian, Justin Bieber, Ellen DeGeneres, LeBron James, Oprah, Trump, Stephen Curry, Adele, your teacher, mom, dad, etc. all went through it and survived.
3. Stick together and support each other because it's all weird and unpredictable. Just be kind, spread warm fuzzies whenever you can.
4. Parents will embarrass you and find this time of your life *"novel."* I know it's odd, but true. Just roll with it.
5. A bra fitting is when they measure a young girl or a woman under her arms and across her chest with a soft measuring tape to determine her bra size. Tip- NEVER have a bra fitting from the mom of the cutest boy in your school.
6. Pick a cute makeup bag to hold your pads and tampons. Bedazzle it if you want to. I can hook you up with the Queen of Bedazzle, my one and only, Glamma.
7. Have a bag of tampons and pads at both of your parents' houses if they are divorced.

8. Blotchy skin may appear around your period. Be sure to wash your face every night and take a shower after sports. Only you will think your zits look like mountains.
9. Toothpaste on your zits kinda works in a pinch. Just be sure to wipe it off before you leave the house.
10. Nobody wants to be the first kid to go through puberty or the last kid. Be understanding of everyone. You do not get to pick your time.
11. Bras do not come with manuals. DON'T figure it out for the first time alone. It may be dangerous. Take your mom or a close friend who knows what they are doing.
12. Chill out and stop making this weird. It is what it is.
13. You will survive this.

There. Now *that* is a complete list.

I rolled over and grabbed my trusty pink diary.

Dear Diary,

Wow, this has been a week of survival! I aged more this past week than I have in over eleven years. Don't get me wrong, I am still a little confused with what is happening to my body, why my brain goes to mush, and why my knees feel weak around Chet. Hubba. Hubba.

The only *thing I know for sure is faking that you know what is going on gets old really fast and it's exhausting.*

Here's a shocker – I finally got the nerve up to ask mom when she had her period. Watson said it can help figure out when I might get mine. I didn't know that asking her would turn into a fiasco of events from bra strangulation to a stained short public humiliation ordeal, to flashing lights at Target, but in the end, I survived it.

Barely.

Mrs. Watson, Mom, and Lily are my puberty lifesavers. I don't know what I would do without them. Lily saved the day at the mall and she only asked that I pay-it-forward.

After heavy debate, I decided that Pesty Peyton can be the benefactor of my pay-it-forward promise and my hard-learned life lessons. Peyton will owe me big time for sharing my puberty guide and my priceless Maddi-isms with her in a couple of years. I mean BIG TIME.

I am going to make Peyton promise to name her first born after me before I hand the goods over to her. Okay, I know technically that's not paying it forward, if I want something in return, but PP can be fun to mess with. It's worth a shot and 'Madison the second' has a nice ring to it.

I really hope that I don't keep stumbling through life from one clueless adventure to the next. It would be great if there were Mrs. Watson's strategically placed throughout my life to throw me a lifeline when I need it. But realistically, if I were a little more chill and tried to see the sunny side of situations again, it probably will get a lot easier.

OMG!! The most important news of all is that CHET is having an end-of-the year, kick-off summer pool party. Everyone is talking about who is dating who and who is going with who to the party. I am going to go with Shelby. That is always a safe bet.

As far as the dating thing goes, I've decided that I'm gonna boycott it. I'm gonna leapfrog the entire dating process until I'm maybe sixty-ish and in the bedazzling everything stage of life. I think that is a solid plan. BOYcott.

I'm well aware that I have never *navigated leap-frogging anything successfully in my entire life. I guess it's my mojo.*

P.S. Growing up is kinda scary and exciting at the same time.

P.P.S. No matter what age I am, I probably will always feel younger on the inside than I actually am, and that, I've decided is a cool thing.

P.P.P.S. What on earth do I wear to Chet's end-of-year party? Obviously, not white shorts. Dah!

Over & out,

Diva of Puberty Survival

Maddie

I closed my diary and tossed it onto my desk. I noticed a pink Post-it Note floating off my desk towards the floor. I grabbed it mid-air. It was a bedazzled pink note with a handwritten message on it.

Sweetness,

I left you a little present in the freezer.

XOX,

Glamma

Yes, SCORE!! It had to be my favorite superman ice cream from Flapdoodles. She's the best! I ran down the hall, slid down the railing, sped to the freezer, and opened it. There was a pink and white gift bag with a dangling bedazzled tag. I grabbed the bag and noticed it is too light to be ice cream. I read the gift tag.

Sweetness,

Use these cold bedazzled cabbage leaves inside your bra to relieve breast soreness.

XOX,

Glamma

<u>YOU</u> ARE PAYING IT FORWARD!

A portion of every book sale will be donated to Days for Girls International. Today you have helped other girls like you going through puberty in a big way by providing much needed menstruation kits and health education. WAY COOL!

Research has found that many girls throughout the world miss school several days a month due to personal discomfort and the potential embarrassment associated with the lack of menstrual products and other basic resources. Many have to resort to using old rags, grass, socks, plastic and paper due to lack of availability.

Menstrual hygiene and health education is a key component of empowering women and girls around the world. Days for Girls is an organization that brings greater dignity, knowledge, and health to more than **1.7 million** women and girls in **144+ countries.** Together, we're creating a world with dignity, health, and opportunity for all girls and women.

For more ideas on how to help girls on the same journey check out www.kellyolsonbooks.com or www.daysforgirls.org.

Thank you for changing lives!

Chill Out & Stop Making This Weird

By Kelly Olson

DISCUSSION

In Chapter One, Maddie *Chicken's Out* from skipping school to avoid the puberty test and from having to reveal her first acne break out. Watching Netflix, junking out on Glamma bread, eating ice cream, and letting Mount St. Helen settle down for a day seems enticing. Do you think she made the right choice or did it just happen so fast that she didn't realize her choice was made by following her daily routine until it was too late? What would you have done?

Do you wish you had an *Anonymous Question Box* where you could put questions about life and someone would answer them for you without knowing you were asking them? What are some of the questions you would ask?

In the *Lying Non-Perioder* chapter, Maddie struggles with, *"Integrity= doing what is right, even when it's hard,"* when confronted with an uncomfortable question in front of her peers. Do you feel she did the right thing by first answering with "Yes," followed by correcting it to a "No?" Describe a time when you experienced something similar regarding integrity.

What was your favorite *Project Schmodject* lesson in chapter four? Why? What is something new you learned regarding nutrition, grooming, exercise, acne, or about friendship through the class presentations?

Why does Maddie decide to keep the cotton ball that Chet gave her when she was supposed to say something kind or perform a kind deed to someone else and pass it on? Why did she break the rules?

In *Late Bloomer* Maddie dreaded asking her mom about when she had her first period. Do you or have you dreaded having conversations with your parents about topics like these? What would make it easier?

In the *Bra Fitting* chapter, Maddie feels anxious about watching for signs of her period and having to go through purchasing her first bra. Do you or have you felt anxious about your period or having to experience new things in unchartered territory? What are some things you can do to relieve feeling nervous?

In chapter seven, Mrs. Watson states, "*Knowledge* comes from understanding the facts about puberty, but my friends, *wisdom* comes from experience, and *intelligence* is having the ability to adjust to the changes involved with the experience or in this case, puberty."

What would you have written on the paper and handed into Mrs. Watson?

Glamma loves life and is *"original"* as Maddie describes her. Do you have someone in your life like Glamma who keeps things light-hearted and is a rock in your life? Do you have someone to talk to if you need them? Who is that and how does that feel to have a confidant if you need one? If you don't feel like you have a person that you can turn to, consider reaching out to your parents, teachers, school nurse, or school counselor and ask for help with this. They are all there to help and like Maddie said, "*Not exactly an easy step, but worth the leap.*"

Are there times when your parents are cool one minute and the next minute you think they are trying to "*make your life difficult,*" as Maddie experienced? Do you think they are truly trying to make your life difficult or are there things you may not understand at the moment and they have experience to better guide you?

In chapter ten, Maddie catches herself thinking the worst about Mia, Brianna, and Lily when she was in line waiting for her food order at Potbelly's at the mall. The girls were trying to figure out how to approach her and the *Unannounced Friend* situation without embarrassing Maddie. Tell about a time where you caught yourself thinking the worst, when actually it wasn't like that at all.

Maddie's mom shares an intimate story about her puberty years with Maddie at the food court. Have you asked your parents about their puberty experience? Do you want to know? Why or why not?

List one or two things that you learned from *Mrs. Watson's life lesson email.*

If you were to add to the *Maddie-ism* list, what would it say?

About the Author

Kelly's love for teaching was fueled for over two decades by her student's daily supply of humor, wit, and their unbridled quest to understand the mysteries of life. She was unable to find light-hearted, relatable books for her students that addressed intimate and complex topics such as menstruation and puberty. *Chill Out & Stop Making This Weird: A Girl's Survival Guide Extraordinaire* was written to fill that void and provide a framework to navigate the ups and downs of adolescence through a fun-loving character who is sharing the same journey.

You can find her at **kellyolsonbooks.com.**

Please consider writing a review. It helps books fall into the hands of young readers. Thank you so much!

Made in the USA
Middletown, DE
25 July 2020

13699625R00084